STRANGER IN THE SMOKE

Action Sweet Romance

Written by: C. L. Hamilton

Stranger in the Smoke

First Edition, Copyright © 2025 Christine Hamilton

Pages N More.com

Written by: Christine Hamilton

Cover designed by: Christine Hamilton

Main figure from: https://www.vecteezy.com/free-photos/fireman.

ISBN: 978-1-7637167-3-5

C.L. Hamilton

This book is dedicated to my emergency services friends
I have made over my twenty-seven years of service.

CHAPTER 1

HOT UNDER THE COLLAR

Sometimes when things get too heated, flames result. *The problem with being a female firefighter married to the job is that everyone becomes just another stranger in the smoke. Figures all dressed the same, their details blurred by a smelly grey-brown mist wafting in the air. And everyone is too busy preventing an unfolding disaster to remember names and faces. Finding a partner is equally as difficult as I am just one of the guys. And if my captain promotion comes through my chances of finding a bloke wanting to date a female firefighter captain is unlikely. Sure, the crews trust each other and have fun together, but most are not partner material.*

With Troy falling ill at the last wildfire deployment, it's been a quiet week with a team member down. Lieutenant Blake Davis breathed deeply as she heaved the weights above her chest. A fellow firefighter from her crew stood over her acting as a spotter for her weight training session. "One more," she grunted, her muscles burning as she pushed the bar higher. With the bar stowed away, she took a deep breath as she sat up and wiped the sweat from her face. *I shouldn't overdo it; we have our second deployment tomorrow.* Looking across at the dark office in the corner of the fire station.

Captain John and his crew will be back in the morning and then we will be off to Brook Hill. I haven't seen Troy's replacement yet. Draping the towel over her shoulder, she reached into her kit bag and grabbed her water bottle. Her shirt clung to her sweaty back as she moved. *Oh, I need a shower and some lunch.* Pulling the shirt away from her skin, she rose turning toward the bathroom.

Captain Bosham or Bo as the crew call him walked into the gym with a stranger at his side. "Everyone, this is Tim Smythe. He will be replacing Troy for this deployment. He has just left the army fire brigade."

OMG. Where did they find him?

The crew gathered to greet their new team member. Tim strode over to the crew, forcefully shaking the bloke's hands. He paused lowering his arm as he looked back at Blake, "Hi," he muttered.

Hi, is that all you can say? She held out her hand, "Lieutenant Blake Davis but call me Blake." Tim briefly made eye contact; his crushing grip stung her hand more than weight lifting. The veins popped between the stretch marks on his pumped-up arm muscles. His puffed-up body was as unappealing as his closely shaved head and piercing eyes. *Ease up on the steroids, Tim. A gorilla might fancy you.* Tim followed Bo back to his office with little to say to anyone.

The crew looked stunned as their eyes darted around the group. "It's going to be one of those weeks," Blake murmured as she headed toward the bathroom.

Fresh from her shower, she joined the others in the lunchroom. Tim was chatting away to the blokes. *He seems to be fitting in.* Grabbing her sandwich from the fridge, she sat beside Bo.

"Blake has been here five years. She is due for a promotion to Captain at the end of the year," Bo said, stirring his coffee.

"Five years, I'll be Captain before then," Tim muttered not lifting his head, and taking a mouthful of his steamed chicken. The crew all looked back at each other in silence.

Not if you continue to be an ass. She glanced across at her crew from under her brow. *That comment doesn't deserve a response.*

One crew member got the message and asked, "Have you seen the new movie—" All conversation was drowned out when the fire siren echoed through the station.

And I just started my lunch. Taking mouthfuls of her sandwich Blake pulled her fire jacket over her shoulder. She reached for the front passenger door handle but Tim was already sitting in the front. *Just take my seat.*

🚒 🚒

The narrow street lined with parked cars on each side made manoeuvring the fire engine difficult. Everyone peered out the side windows checking on clearances as the truck crawled along. Eventually arriving at the scene, they pulled into a driveway, the back half of the fire engine partly blocked the road. A civilian had accidentally set alight to their shed while welding. Flames licked the walls and smoke poured from the roof.

"Blake on hose one," Bo ordered with his head in the switchboard checking that the power was off to the shed.

"I'll take that, you man the radio," Tim butted in grabbing the hose. Only feet away, his shoulder almost hit hers as his hands tried to push hers aside.

Blake resisted his grip and ordered, "Start up the pump." *I will not react in public. At least one of us can be professional.* Tim

3

tugged the hose again before she glared back at him, "Find the street hydrant and connect it to the truck," she ordered sternly.

"Bloody woman taking over," Tim mumbled as he disappeared behind the truck.

What did he say? She paused, her eyes widening as her anger grew. *Focus on the fire.* Her neck stiffened as she went back to the task at hand.

With the fire extinguished, Blake placed the equipment in the truck. Closing a hatch, she noticed Tim and Bo were having a heated moment behind the engine. She didn't pay much attention to the argument and kept rolling up the hoses. *It doesn't involve me.* Carrying out a final check of the yard she returned to hear her name being yelled out by one of them as they argued with each other. *What? I hope the deployment is not going to be like this.*

It wasn't just the fire suit making her hot under the collar. Tim had made several derogatory comments throughout the task. The trip back to the station was quiet as she stared out the back passenger window. She shuffled in her seat as the shadow of the station garage roof ran over the truck as it reversed home. *Right. Time to stop this crap.*

Gathering her gear, she took a deep breath, her jaw clenched as Tim started throwing orders the moment his feet hit the floor. Putting all her focus into staying silent was her only means of controlling her rising anger. Climbing from the fire truck she didn't get time to remove her jacket when Tim ordered her to refill the drinking water. *That does it! I'm second in charge here.* Blake ripped off her jacket tossing it behind her and spun around to face Tim, "You are not in charge here," she glared over her finger as she waved it in his face, "And if you ever belittle me in public again." Her voice rose above the station noise.

Tim shoved his face closer to hers, only inches away, his sour breath drowned out the smell of burnt plastic in his clothing, "Women aren't strong enough to handle firehoses!" His overpowering yell went hoarse as his face turned a dark shade of red.

What the! Her neck stiffened as she glared back at him. *I'm not taking your macho BS.* She took a deep breath and braced herself, "Get out of my face!" She reached out, giving him a huge shove. Unprepared for her reaction he stumbled backward. The thud of his body hitting the steel truck door matched his groan.

He bounced back to his feet and lunged forward with his palm raised. His glare locked with hers.

"Whoa. Calm down," a crew member called out from behind the truck. The crew dropped their gear and rushed toward the two of them.

"Blake! Stand down," Bo ordered stepping in between them with his arm out ready to block any retaliation. "Go for a shower."

She stood her ground, glaring back at Tim. "Now!" Bo ordered blocking her view with his chest. With Bo standing so close, she stepped back looking at Bo's less than impressed gaze. Turning away, she ground her teeth and strode toward the showers. *If he had hit me, he would have needed an ambulance. And I wouldn't have been the cause of his injuries.*

Closing the bathroom door, she peeled her sweaty shirt over her head. The muffled yelling could be heard through the wall. Turning the shower up and letting the hot water run over her head deadened some of the argument outside. *Why wasn't he shot in the army? Surely there were women there who thought about it.*

The team was not the same after that fight. It was shut up and get the job done. Everyone was concerned about starting another argument. There were some private conversations, but the team interaction was cold and toxic.

With the shift over the crew had gone home, leaving Blake and Bo at the station. Blake still fuming from the afternoon's events, packed her kit for the return trip to the wildfire at Brook Hill. Bo silently walked past her carrying a box to the truck. "Couldn't we leave him behind and find a replacement on site?" She asked.

"We don't have time to replace him."

"Do we need him?"

"Yes, unfortunately," Bo dipped his head as he lowered the side compartment hatch. The door didn't shut, resulting in some forceful shoves on the contents before the latch closed.

"Well, if you don't control him, I will," she replied sternly, zipping up her bag and loading it in the truck.

"Don't get dragged into his crap. Remember who you are," Bo's voice softened as he returned to his office, looking back from the doorway, he ordered, "Go home, get some sleep."

🚒 🚒

Blake sat alone in the booth at the pub staring back at the ice floating in her drink. A wall light overhead dimly lit up the stained table top. Her thoughts played out scenarios for removing Tim from the deployment. *Call the police, an injury, or put laxatives in his breakfast.* She twirled the glass between her fingers when her phone buzzed. *Trish.* "We are at the bar."

"Look left." Blake texted back, straightening her posture. Peering through the dim light. *She brought her boyfriend to a girl's night? And what's with the little red dress?*

Blake looked up at the couple standing at the end of the table, "You said seven. It's a quarter to eight. And why are you dressed all fancy for the pub?"

Trish sat across the table and outstretched her fingers, "We were late because Jim proposed."

Taking hold of her hand, Blake leaned over to examine the ring, "Congratulations. It's big." *It has to be a fake diamond.*

Jim sat beside Trish and looked around the bar "Where is your partner?"

Ha. "Single," Blake replied with a flat tone sipping her drink.

"Well, you won't find one here dressed in cargo pants and an office shirt," Trish said, leaning over the table. "Is that vodka?"

"Yeah," Blake moaned.

Trish turned to Jim, "Give us a minute. She is drinking vodka."

"So," he replied, looking back confused.

"Bad day," she whispered over his shoulder.

"Oh," he rose and went back to the bar.

Placing her purse to the side, Trish asked, "Should you be drinking? Don't you have a deployment tomorrow?"

"Why are you drinking rum and cola? What happened to your zero carb fitness goals," Blade asked taking the last mouthful of vodka.

"Celebrating our engagement," Trish leaned towards Blake and murmured, "What has happened?"

Blake dropped her gaze, "A stressful day."

"Find a man to ease your frustrations?" Trish replied taking a sip of her drink.

Ease my frustrations, ha, they are the cause. "When do I get time to meet blokes?"

7

Lunging forward Trish dropped her elbows on the table, "You work in a sea of men. Firefighters at that."

"Why do you think I'm drinking? I thumped an asshole today," Blake muttered still fiddling with her glass.

Shocked by the answer, Trish moved around the table, sitting beside Blake, "Thumped a bloke. Go, girl. Not the way I would get a bloke but if it works."

Date Tim! Blake shifted back in the seat, her eyes wide, "Get stuffed. I want to kill him, not date him." Blake waved at a passing waiter.

Trish glanced up as the waiter arrived, "A jug of water please." Turning back to Blake, "Fires and hangovers don't mix. Don't worry about him, surely you can find nice blokes you can have a coffee with."

"Have you seen them? It's all sweaty socks and body odour."

Pouring a glass of ice water, Trish replied, "You probably aren't much better at work."

"Go find Jim, focus more on your love life and less on mine," Blake sculled the water, "I'm heading home for some sleep."

CHAPTER 2

STRANGER IN THE SMOKE

Up at dawn, tired but ready for the day ahead, Blake sat silently in Bo's office sipping her takeaway coffee. Facing away from the window, she distanced herself from the crew carrying out final checks on the truck. Tim's voice stood out above the others as he barked orders. "I will kill him if he starts on me. I'm not taking his crap all week," she whispered, staring down at her cup.

Bo had his back to her, focusing on loading his kit bag when he murmured, "Focus on the task. Ignore him, think of your promotion." He dug around in his desk, "Have you seen my knife? I put it in my drawer yesterday."

"No, I haven't been in your drawer."

He opened a few more drawers, the contents rattled as he dug around. "I need that too," he muttered shoving something in his pocket, he held up the knife, "Found it."

The noise of the crew chatter changed to the clanging of steel hatches shutting on the truck. All fell silent when a crew member stuck his head through the doorway, "Ready to go."

Bo threw his bag over his shoulder, pausing beside Blake as she rose, "Talk to me before you kill him." Turning toward the door, he whispered, "So I can ensure there are no witnesses." He smiled and kept walking and calling back, "Blake, are you coming?"

Arriving at the truck, Blake looked up to Tim sitting in the front passenger seat. *There's a surprise.*

Bo climbed in the driver's seat and buckled his seatbelt, "I need Blake in the front to navigate."

Oh, my god. Did he just say that? Kicking Tim out of the front seat so I can navigate. Ha. It's the same camp as last time, he knows how to get there. Blake waited on the passenger side as Tim climbed out of the truck muttering. She stared ahead, ignoring his glare. Glancing at Bo, she pulled herself up into the seat. He looked forward, not reacting as he started the engine.

A line of fire appliances snaked through the traffic heading for Brook Hill. Blake silently gazed out the windscreen. *Let's hope this week is over quickly.* The only chatter in the cabin came from the fire communications radio.

After a two-hour drive, they arrived at a large football field away from the firefront. Their fire truck joined a long line of trucks parked on the grass verge. At one end of the field sat two mid-sized helicopters and at the other end a large tent city beside the football club building. A city made up of rows of tents of various sizes each with a specific purpose, sleeping, communications, operations and feeding the hoard. The football club opened up their showers and toilets for the operation.

The blue sky to the west had been replaced with towering columns of grey smoke. Blake walked into the same tent as last time, ten empty stretchers covered the floor. Tossing her kit on her camp stretcher, she was greeted by an unknown firefighter. *We have a different team sleeping with us this week, I hope they don't snore too.*

Bo stuck his head in the tent doorway, "Be in Fire Ops in five minutes."

⛟ ⛟

Little time was wasted getting the crews in the field. Bo's crew's first mission involved joining other crews and preparing an outer suburb for the approaching flames. Every breath hurt with the Forty-degree hot dry winds blowing over the hills. The whole environment was baked to the point of spontaneous combustion.

Blake gathered her kit and wiped her brow. *I'm going to turn into a dehydrated prune.* A salty taste entered her mouth every time she licked her dry lips. Her feet ached on the rocky ground as she pushed on clearing fire breaks and back-burning small areas.

Support crews rode by on quad bikes, visiting each crew with boxes of bottled water and food. The problem came when there wasn't enough staff to keep up the hydration needs of the crews. Getting hit with the back spray of a fire hose was refreshing, as long as you didn't think about where the water came from.

Tim was trying to prove something to Bo, by jumping in and being the first to do everything. Blake walked ahead focused on clearing a fire break and blocking out Tim as much as possible.

Bo called out, "Blake, continue along that fence."

He is trying to keep us separated. Is that for my peace of mind or his? Blake moving along property boundaries brought every dog to their back fences. Some were happier than others to see her. Saying hello to the friendly dogs broke the tension created by the unfriendly dogs trying to jump their fences. The gnashing teeth through the bars increased her grip on her fire rake as she stepped aside.

Glancing back over her shoulder her team worked away behind her while other teams were dotted around the area. All wearing similar protective clothing, helmets and masks, making it difficult to recognise anyone in the wafts of smoke created by the back burning. Sighing, she enjoyed some personal time while working towards other teams. However, the peace was not to last as Tim's grating voice came over the radio, "Blake, roll up the spare hoses."

You are closer to the truck than I am, you do it. Keeping her head down, she took a deep breath and kept walking. *Would they notice if he went missing on the fire ground?* After clearing a pile of dead branches, she leaned back against a tree sculling a mouthful of water. Taking a moment to cool down, she scanned the paddock. Unknown firefighters were scurrying around everywhere. Sirens would come and go. In the distance, helicopters buzzed back and forth, each dropping water on the flaming hills. All the while the fire front marched onward.

Tim called out as he approached, "You haven't rolled up the hoses yet."

Blake glanced back from under her brow. "Go f... yourself," she muttered, pushing off from the tree and walking toward the other firefighters.

"I gave you an order," Tim yelled across the grassland.

Oh, lord keep me from whacking him. Blake's fists firmly gripped the rake handle as she powered toward a nearby crew. She glanced at a firefighter who had looked up at the yelling. Her eyes connected with his, lingering briefly before she turned away. Something about him had caught her eye, but she was in no mood to work it out. Holding back her frustration brought her to the verge of tears. *Keep walking.* She wanted to unleash but didn't want to destroy her promotion hopes. *As Captain, I would rather have a man down than have him in my team. He is an added hazard.*

Further along the fire break, she was joined by the same crew she had made eye contact with earlier. A tall figure came alongside, with a quick side glance, he had the same dusty outfit. *A captain?* He casually walked beside her, holding out a bag of gummy bear lollies, "Is everything Okay?" He asked in a deep concerned voice.

She glanced over her shoulder and muttered, "What do you think?"

He paused looking back at her as she said nothing more, "I think not. Who is that guy? He is not a Captain."

"Just a prick, the boss found somewhere." She turned away and kept walking calling back, "I don't want to talk about him."

The captain hurried up beside her, "Peter Sycamore," he held out his hand with a friendly smile.

Those blackened gloves have seen too many fires. "Blake Davis," she replied with a weary smile. His handshake was sincere and friendly.

His eyes were drawn to her jacket, "Highgate Station. One of us."

I have never seen you before. She glanced down at the name on his jacket. *Mansell Station.* "Us? You mean the other side of the city."

He held out the lollies again, "Take one." She returned a smile as she pulled a candy from the packet.

Later that night, a new shift had replaced Peter's crew on the fire-front. The tents were dark except for a few lamps in the kitchen and mess. Blake tossed and turned. Her tent rattled with a range of snoring tones. *Stuff this.* Muttering to herself, she dragged her aching body out of bed, pulled on her boots and headed outside.

Grabbing a cup of tea from the mess she wandered toward the carpark. Flopping down beside a fire truck, the rubber tyre offered some padding for her back. Alone in the darkness, it was relatively quiet. The camp was far enough away from the action that she couldn't hear the sirens that haunted her work life.

A glowing curtain framed the distant hills and red lights flew back and forth across the night sky. Her flashlight sat between her feet reflecting off the nearby truck. Needing some relaxation, she flicked through her phone and pulled up her favourite music. She inserted her earpiece, dropped her head, closed her eyes and let the tension melt away with each slow breath.

"Can I join you?" A deep calm voice came from the darkness.

Her heart skipped a beat as she jumped, flicking her flashlight toward the voice. "Peter?" She removed her earpiece," Sure." *Who sent him over to check on me?* "What's up?"

"I saw your light. Someone could have been up to no good." His towering silhouette stood out at the end of the truck, "What brings you over here?" He asked.

"The peace. Have a seat," she replied, patting the ground beside her.

He eased down next to her and she shuffled sideways to give him room on the tyre. "How was your day?" He asked.

"You were there, you saw how great it was," she muttered, rolling her flashlight in her palms. The grass in the light beam had her attention as she fought to stay calm.

"Anything you want to talk about?" He asked in a gentle tone.

She shook her head, "It's not your problem." Her chest tightened as she fought to control her rising emotions.

He shuffled, straightening his back, "Well, I think he is an arrogant ass. He wouldn't last five minutes in my crew," his voice softened. "I saw how he talked to you. Why doesn't Bosham do something?"

"He tried but they just started arguing. Tim was a last-minute stand-in. I want him gone," taking a deep breath, "Work used to be enjoyable before he joined the crew. Now we can't get out of the truck fast enough." Tears welled in her eyes. She fell silent except for the occasional sniffle.

"Don't let him get to you." Peter's soft voice offered her more support than she had felt all day.

I wish. Wiping her tears on her sleeve, "I'm due for a promotion to Captain. I don't want him destroying it for me."

"Don't worry. I'll back you." The gentle touch of his hand on her arm made her pulse increase.

"Thanks," her cheeks flushed, "I will remember that." *The more help the better. He doesn't even know me.* She glanced back over her shoulder. *It's dark, I don't know him either.*

"Don't sell yourself short. You'll get there," he replied.

"With no help from that prick."

"What do you like doing for fun outside of work?" He asked holding out a bag of boiled lollies.

More lollies. She glanced back with a smile, taking a candy, "Movies or getting outdoors, fishing."

"Freshwater or reef?"

"Anything. It clears my head." His distraction was working as the pain in her chest eased.

After an hour of chatting about their favourite fishing spots and some laughs, he tapped her shoulder, "We should get some sleep."

"They all snore."

"The end tent is empty. Use that," he replied, getting to his feet, holding out his hands and helping her up off the ground.

Partway back to the tents, he broke away, "See you around."

"Maybe," Blake replied. Slowly wandering back to camp, Peter's silhouette vanished into the darkness. Sneaking back into the tent she grabbed her sleeping bag and headed for a peaceful night of slumber.

CHAPTER 3

TEAM CHANGE

Refreshed from a quiet night's sleep, Blake sat alone at a mess table. She looked up from her sausage and egg breakfast taking a sip from her cup. *Eww. Do they call this coffee? It's better than nothing I suppose.* She silently panned the early morning crowd. Some handle the dawn rises better than others. *It will take more than this coffee to erase the bags under those eyes.*

The camp was alive with activity. A few of the younger fitter firefighters returned from a jog, and others were ready for the day ahead. Peter and Bo loaded equipment at the store, talking to each other with their back to the camp. Some blokes loaded their plates with everything on the buffet. *I'm glad I don't have a male appetite; my shopping list would drain my bank account.*

Troy sat across from her, reaching out for the barbeque sauce. "Where were you this morning?"

"I got up early for a jog," she murmured, gripping her fork firmly.

"I was up at four and your stretcher was empty."

Is he my father, checking I'm not out with the boys? She sighed and looked back at him, "I needed space, I can't—" Tim and the other crew members crowded the table. Pausing she glanced back to Troy as she rose, "I have to get new shoes before we go." She grabbed her plate and headed for the kitchen.

Back in the tent, she rushed to adjust her jacket and grabbed her kit. Reaching for her helmet, she muttered, "Get this day over with."

On her way to the carpark, Bo stepped out from behind a vehicle, and panned the area, "Can we talk?"

What with the covert stuff? She followed him behind a truck where they met with Peter and another muscly firefighter in full uniform. *What is going on?* Her eyes darted around the group.

"We are swapping you over for the rest of the deployment. Clyde will replace you in our team," Bo said.

That would be bloody right. Blake rolled her eyes and glared at Bo, "Tim is the problem, so I have to move?" *Get rid of him.*

"It's temporary. You will be happier in my team," Peter replied.

She looked up at Clyde towering over her, "And what did he do wrong to be punished."

Peter grinned, "Clyde can look after himself. Welcome to the Mansell crew, Blake."

🚒 🚒

While the day was hot and sweaty it passed quickly and was nowhere near as stressful. The crew accepted me as one of the team, I don't have to keep an eye out for Tim. It was still an exhausting day but the sour team toxicity was gone. Upon returning to camp, she silently moved her kit to the new crew tent. Looking around at the group of strangers she introduced herself and asked, "Do any of you snore?"

"Sorry," one bloke replied.

"I'll grab you some earplugs from the store," added another.

Earplugs why didn't I think of that? She pulled out her shower bag from her kit. *What is that?* Something caught her eye between the stretcher and the tent wall. Balancing one hand on the stretcher she reached over pulling out a dirty sock with her two fingers. Her bottom lip curled in disgust as she flung the sock towards the bin. Wiping her fingers on her dirty pants, she muttered, "Phew. Who cleaned this tent after the last changeover?" *I definitely need a shower now.*

Walking back across the paddock the blood-red sunset gave the place a Mars quality. Feeling refreshed her wet hair no longer smelled of smoke. Peter passed her partway back to the tent, "Want to join us at the pub for dinner?"

Hell yeah. "Give me a minute," she replied, rushing toward the tent. Her tired body regained some energy as she tied back her long hair. Stepping out of the tent, she spun around, "My phone."

The crew waited in a four-wheel drive vehicle as she hurried toward the carpark. Jumping into the back seat, the poor guy in the middle had to pull his shoulders inward as she searched for the seat-belt buckle. Peter was in the driver's seat focusing on the road as the chatter continued. The pain of her aching muscles could not remove the smile on her face. *I could get used to this.*

The sun had dropped behind the smoky hills. While the carpark security lights were dim, the lighting at the front of the pub lit up the walkway. Blakes clothes clung to her sweaty back in the hot night air. Walking through the front door the air-conditioning was a welcome luxury. Keen for a cold drink, the group headed for the bar, chatting and laughing. Blake chuckled at a teasing joke. Upbeat music played in the background. Patrons sat around enjoying themselves. Her pulse slowed as a grin grew on her face. *Should I apply for a transfer to Mansell Station?*

In the light, her eyes ran over the crew. All around six foot tall, their faces lightly covered in stubble each wearing a different style. *They look so different out of uniform and having washed off the dirt and sweat. Looking at their casual clothing, you would never say firefighter. Thou, short back and sides give them away. They all seem to use the same barber.*

Peter approached the bar, "Our table is in the back room."

An overhead light cast a warm glow over his face. That chiselled jaw and his warm smile brought out the dimples on his cheeks. His hair was longer than the others like he missed their last barber visit. *Wow, he looks good. The darkness and grime had hidden his best features to date. Even when he had his helmet off at lunch, his face had a black tinge. His clean sandy brown looks better than dark slicked down with sweat look. Though his warm brown eyes are lost in the bloodshot whites. Red from salty sweat and smoke. He can't be much older than I am.*

A group of five at the table still had an intimate feeling. Blake glanced over the top of the menu, briefly making eye contact with Peter before looking at the bar menu. "I'm getting drinks, what do you all want?"

"We should be buying you a drink," Peter replied.

"No, you have been more than welcoming. Let me return the favour." A rumble ran around the table, "Four pints of ale." *Easy to remember.*

Peter rose with her, "I'll help you carry them back." Weaving through the crowd he wasn't far behind her. He leaned on the bar waiting for the bartender, and glanced over his shoulder, "Was today better than yesterday?"

"Oh, God yes." Smiling, her eyes connected with his briefly before he turned away. Her gaze lingered silently taking in his body language. *He seems as self-conscious as I am.*

🚒 🚒

The social mood continued around the table, as the crew ate dinner. Blake looked down at her plate groaning under the weight of the crumbed steak draped over her vegetables. *Is that the whole cow? I see why the blokes like coming here.*

"So, Blake, how's life in your home team?" A crew member asked, cutting up his steak. He jumped glancing toward Peter as a dull thud came from under the table.

Don't destroy a good night. Blake glanced up at Peter before looking back at her plate. "When do you think we will have these fires under control?" She asked.

"I don't know. Hopefully, before we head home on Friday," Peter replied wiping his hands on a napkin.

A waiter stopped at the various fire crew's tables, "Is anyone ordering dessert?"

Dessert? I can't fit in dinner. "Just a coffee for me," she replied.

The crew kept chatting away eating their dessert. Blake sat back in her seat relaxing. *This team bonds well. Peter is still a strong leader and they all respect each other. Is he single? What would he be like as a partner? It would be interesting to find out.* Observing the group dynamics she silently sipped her coffee. *Oh, they are sharing their desserts around the table. Makes it easy if you can't decide what to order.*

Peter looked back at her holding out his plate, "Are you sure you don't want any ice cream? I haven't touched it."

"No, thank you." *I bet he has a girlfriend. What woman would let him get away?*

🚒 🚒

The camp was dark when they returned. After an enjoyable night out, Blake grabbed a bottle of water from the mess and wandered towards the carpark. Silently walking past her tent, she stepped out into the darkness.

Peter was chatting with the guys when he glanced over his shoulder, "I have left my phone in the car."

Heading toward the carpark, the southerly change had arrived, and a cool breeze blew in from the other end of camp. *This will slow the fire spread.* She leaned against the front of a fire truck, her eyes tracking a lone figure approaching through the darkness. "I was wondering when I would see you," she said.

"You were waiting for me?"

"I saw you put your phone in your pocket."

Peter leaned back beside her. Their shoulders almost touching, he turned his face towards her, "What's the problem?"

"Nothing, I'm not tired. Let's go for a walk."

The night air was peaceful, a pleasant change from the hot cha-otic fire ground. *Strolling in the darkness with a guy I have only known for twenty-four hours would freak out some people but he has a calming energy. Nothing about him is threatening.* Reaching the far end of the field, she sat on a grassy mound. Turning off her torch she looked back over the camp. A city of tents, generators, and trucks partly lit by solar panels and batteries, while the helicopters sat quietly in the foreground.

"Do you enjoy the darkness?" He asked, standing off to the side.

"Yes, it adds to the peace."

Navigating in the dark, Peter brushed her arm as he sat beside her, "I hope the football team isn't upset with the tent peg holes in the turf."

"Yeah, the East Lakes cricket club wasn't happy last year." *How many times have I looked back at this setup?* She silently paused, "I sometimes wonder why I rent an apartment at this time of year. I'm never home."

"Who's looking after your pets?" He asked.

"You mean the dead pot plant on my kitchen table. No one, I live alone."

"No family or partner?" He casually asked.

Oh, just ask me if I am single. "Nope, I'm single. How about you?"

"Same. My mother is still alive and in a retirement home." He turned towards her, "If work gets too stressful back home, you're welcome to drop by the station for a coffee anytime."

"Thanks, but Tim is only standing in for the deployment. I won't see him after Friday," she replied.

"Even after he is gone, you are still welcome," his voice faded as he silently stared into the darkness.

Taking a deep breath, she gazed back at the fire trucks. "I have never had a problem with the other blokes." Tim's arrogant voice echoed in her thoughts, "He—he makes me, grr." She clenched her fists and twitched jaw muscles.

The gentle touch of Peter's hand on her shoulder eased her tight chest. "Ignore him. Chill, enjoy the good times." He chuckled, "I kicked Alex under the table tonight to keep you happy."

Wow, he is trying to please me. "Well, I thumped Tim before we left home. It didn't make me that happy." Taking a long slow breath. *Change the topic.* "How do you relax after a bad day?"

"Getting outdoors, playing pool, socialising with the guys." A set of vehicle lights left the car park and sped down the road, "Someone needs something important."

"Yeah, I'm glad we are not on the night shift. I can't sleep during the day. It's too bright."

"Speaking of sleep," He patted her back, "If you are Okay. I need some sleep; we have another big day tomorrow."

Wandering back, she leaned closer, his body radiated warmth in the cool night, "Thank you for your support."

"Anytime, I enjoyed the chat."

🚌 🚌

The flames were getting closer to one street. Crews were running around everywhere. The helicopters were dropping water on the flames as hot embers rained down on the nearby houses.

Peter's crew's attention changed from the approaching front to a back yard as low flames in the garden mulch ran up the tree. The embers kept falling over nearby homes. Peter dropped to one knee, holding out his hands and heaved the crew over the back fence. Blake turned to steady him as he pulled himself over the top. Her heart rate matched her stress level as everything got more hectic.

A fire truck pulled up out front. Blake ran down the side of the house to grab a fire hose. Pushing open the gate, she came face to face with Tim. He shoved her aside, "Get out of the way."

Stumbling back into the fence, Blake regained her balance. *What? You bastard.*

She lunged forward when Peter blocked the path shoving his hand into Tim's shoulder, taking a firm grip, he muttered, "You do that again and you won't remember a thing."

Blake froze, eyes wide, looking back at the fierce gaze between the two as Tim pulled his shoulder free and stormed back to the truck. Her eyes locked on Peter's face when he looked back and yelled, "Get a hose."

Right, back to work. Blake stepped aside as a crew member burst through the gate dragging a hose behind them. She arrived on the footpath to see a civilian running down the street yelling and stopping at the Bo's crew. Their neighbour's house further down the street had caught fire. Blake took off running ahead of the others, her pulse pounding as memories of her parent's home burning flooded her thoughts. She lunged forward but had to pull back as the heat at the gate was too fierce to enter. Stepping back and forth, her body jittered when someone threw their arms around her from behind dragging her backward.

"It's empty!" Bo yelled, "They evacuated yesterday."

It took a moment for the news to sink in. Taking a deep breath, Blake slumped in Bo's arms, tears welling in her eyes.

Bo stepped back taking a firm grip of her arms, "There is no one to save here. Pull it together and save someone else."

She paused wiping her face. "I had to check."

"You can't save anyone if you are dead," he replied sternly, "Take a break. You're not thinking straight." Another fire truck roared up beside them. Bo leaned in, "Do that again and you're on leave."

Taking a deep breath as she turned around, Peter stood silent beside Bo's truck, his gaze tracking her as she approached.

Blocking her path, Peter asked, "What was all that about?"

"Nothing. I don't want to talk about it," she pushed past him and disappeared into the backyard.

🚒 🚒

Returning to camp Blake dropped out of the truck, her legs not wanting to hold her up. She returned from the showers and collapsed onto her stretcher. Her stomach grumbled as Peter entered the tent. "You don't look like you want to go the pub."

"Not really."

He looked around at the few crew members with similar energy levels in the tent, "I'll order some pizzas and eat in."

Half an hour later, Ted crouched beside her, and whispered, "Peter said to meet him down past the helicopters."

What's with the Secret Service stuff? "When?"

"Now."

Pulling on her boots, she joined two other crew members on the edge of the darkness. Peter sat on the grass mound, surrounded by pizza boxes and bottles of soft drinks, all lit with a flashlight. "Why are we eating here?" she asked, sitting beside him.

"You walk into a camp full of blokes with pizzas and see how they react," he replied filling his cup.

"Good point. That's why you're the captain."

"Your time will come," he replied, lifting the box lid and pulling out a slice of pizza.

That smells good. She leaned toward his shoulder, "Good going with Tim today."

"He's lucky I was the only one to see him push you. The others wouldn't have been so kind," Peter murmured as he panned the group. He handed her a napkin, "Dig in before they eat it all."

As the evening went on, the crew discussed more personal stuff. Memories of the fire careers, how they met their wives and who had kids. Blake's tired head couldn't remember most of the conversation. One of the guys was not as subtle as Peter and asked "Have you got a boyfriend?"

"I'm not ladylike enough for most blokes. I tell them I'm a firefighter and they leave."

Peter turned his face toward her, "Not all men are like that. Some want someone they can have fun with—like fishing."

Fishing? What is he saying? "Well, if you find one of them send him my way." Her eyes grew heavy, she grabbed Peter's shoulder to steady herself as she rose to her feet. "But not tonight, I need sleep." She wandered back to camp, leaving the crew talking.

CHAPTER 4

SWAMP WATER

Day four of deployment. The action started as soon as the crews arrived on-site. The firefront had turned toward a different suburb. Several crews were working along an overgrown creek behind the houses. The fire reached a thick patch of dry undergrowth further downstream sending flames into the air. Ribbons of burnt grass rained down through the smoky air. Peter's crew cleared the fire break at the back of the houses and Bo's team was further up the creek.

A garbled radio message came from a nearby helicopter. *Oh, crap, a chopper drop.* Those further up the bank ran for the fence line. Blake slumped back against the fence and grabbed her water. The loaded helicopter roared over the tree line. A wall of water rained down over the area where Bo's crew was working.

"Bo!" Blake's heart skipped as she took off towards the creek. Leaning over the edge, the crew looked back drenched and covered in mud from being knocked down the slope. Taking hold of a small tree partway down the bank, she reached out, "Grab my hand." Taking a firm hold of his wrist she strained to keep hold of the tree, her sweaty hands slipped inside her gloves. *Damn this.* Ripping her gloves off in frustration, she tossed them behind her. Taking a deep

28

breath, she gripped Bo's wrist again and heaved as his feet slipped on the muddy slope. Part way up Bo scrambled up the last of the bank. Blake took a deep breath before bracing herself again.

"Give me your hand, I sprained my ankle," Tim called out from a fallen tree.

Not likely. Blake reached out to another teammate leaving Tim for the other crews to rescue. Back on flat ground, Bo offered his thanks. The breeze came from Bo's direction. Blake jumped back covering her nose, "You stink like a fishy swamp."

Bo flicked the mud off his jacket. He looked back developing a wicked grin. Stretching out his arms he stepped forward, "What did you say? You wanted a group hug with your crew?"

Hell no. She jumped backward, "No, bloody way." Bo took another step forward laughing. Blake backtracked, "Get away from me. Help, Peter!"

The interaction was cut short by another radio call from the helicopter. Two firefighters grabbed Tim like a sandbag and dragged him up the bank as everyone evacuated to the fence. A nearby crew noticed Bo's team's swamp odour. One firefighter fired up the truck water pump and rinsed them off. While they looked cleaner, they still had a smell only a dog would love.

Leaning against the fence, everyone had a break as the helicopter kept flooding the area with swamp water. Peter casually pulled up beside Blake, holding out a set of gloves, "Yours I believe."

"Oh, thanks. I was wondering where they went."

🚒 🚒

The day got hotter and sticky. Blake leaned back against a fence post, sculling her cool water. Pouring another bottle over her flushed face, she moaned, "I'm glad we are going home tomorrow." Resting as she took a deep breath, several firefighters worked away in the clouds of smoke. One of them looked in her direction and headed toward her.

Peter flopped back against the fence rail, pulling out his drink bottle, "Big dinner at the pub tonight." He held out a bag of mint lolly crumbs and two wrapped candies. Taking one he held the bag in front of her.

That bag of lollies didn't last long with all these hungry mouths. "What's with you and lollies?" Blake asked taking the last mint.

Peter laughed, "Energy, and it keeps the crew happy."

"I prefer caramels," she replied, sliding her helmet over her sweat-drenched hair.

🚒 🚒

The pub was packed with other fire crews, enjoying their last night together. It wasn't only Peter's crew at the table, two more crews had joined them. Bo dropped by for a drink. Everyone was going over memories of the last few weeks. Some blokes would swear, then look back at Blake wide-eyed and humbly apologise before swearing again moments later. After the third apology, Blake laughed, "Don't worry about it. I've heard worse."

"You have said worse," Alex replied.

"When?"

"Yesterday. When you tripped over that log in the grass."

She tilted her head with a smile, "That bloody hurt."

As the night went on a scuffle broke out in the back corner of the pub but no one paid much attention to it until the police arrived. The loud swearing at the back of the room silenced the crowd. Blake and the crew stared back at Tim struggling with two police officers as he was led away in handcuffs. *Whoa, who has he upset now?* The police walked out the door and the bar noise level rose again.

"Bloody hell," Bo grumped jumping to his feet and taking off for the door. Returning to the table ten minutes later, slipping his phone into his pocket. The bags under his eyes added to his tired face. Shaking his head, he reached for his beer and moaned, "Tim punched the chopper contractor." Everyone's jaw dropped as they stared back at Bo. "Tim complained about being drenched with swamp water and he didn't like the pilot's reply,"

Well, I won't be seeing him again. "Is the pilot all right?" Blake asked.

"Yeah."

While the arrest added chaos to the trip, a tension lifted off her shoulders. The crew raised their glasses, "Cheers."

"It's not that bloody great. I have more paperwork now," Bo replied, placing his empty glass on the table. "I need another drink." Turning to Blake, "You had it easy this trip, you can shout me a pint."

🚒 🚒

Back at camp, the crews enjoyed the night in the canteen. Both crews had come together during the night. Blake scanned the group, Bo and Peter were off doing something else. She grabbed a bottle of water and headed out into the night. Tracking towards the carpark Peter appeared in her torchlight, leaning on the same fire truck as last time.

"Waiting for me?" She asked. "Am I that predictable?"

"Yes." He turned, wandering off down the paddock beside her.

"Well, that's the last time I will see that idiot."

"I said someone would take him out," Peter replied, leaning his head closer to hers. "Are you disappointed it wasn't you?"

Hey, am I going to take this? She lightly thumped her shoulder into his, "What are you saying?" She chuckled. "I wouldn't take him out at work. Too much paperwork and my five-year career would be over." She paused, "Tim can ruin his career without help."

Strolling in the cool night air, Peter asked, "Five years? What made you want to become a firefighter?"

Blake dipped her head, "My parents died in a house fire, six years ago. I couldn't save them." A vision of the neighbours comforting her as her parents' house burned flashed before her eyes. Her voice faded as tension built in her chest and tears welled in her eyes.

Peter's comforting touch rubbed her back, "I'm sorry. Bo told me last night. Is that what happened at the house fire?"

Tears rolled down her face as she fought off the visions. "That house was the same as my folks." After a pause, she straightened up taking a long slow breath, "I became a firefighter to prevent that from happening to anyone else."

His voice softened, "We—we can't save them all."

Her inner soul wanted to hug him so badly. She wiped her cheek, "I know that now. But I have to try."

He turned towards her, "You have to put yourself first. How can you save anyone if you perish with them."

Change the subject. Pausing for a moment, she asked. "How long have you been a firefighter?"

"Nine years, not as long as Bo. He must be hitting fifteen years. He should be retiring soon."

"Bo still has years in him yet." Reaching the end of the field, Blake eased down against a fallen tree trunk; the night air had gone still. "Nine years, what did you do before that?"

"Building inspector and then a fire inspector."

"Wow, you know your buildings."

He nodded, "What job did you have?"

"Site manager for quarry."

"Quarry manager? Don't want to upset you."

She laughed, "Don't forget it." The increasing humidity made her face clammy. *What happened to the southerly change?* The silence of the night gave way to low rumbles of thunder and distant flashes of lighting behind the hills. "Looks like rain," she said, watching multiple ground strikes hit the horizon. *About bloody time, we needed rain three weeks ago.*

"Hopefully, enough to stop the fires," Peter said.

"Yeah, three deployments in two months. I'm ready for some boring city work," she replied. The conversation changed to their memories of the deployments and the laughs flowed.

"What are you looking forward to when you get home? Peter asked stretching out his legs along the ground.

"Getting some peace. Fishing," she leaned towards him, "Give me your phone."

"Why?" He asked slowly pulling it from his pocket.

"To enter my phone number," she held out her hand, "How can we chat back home if you don't have my number?"

"Oh," he swiped the screen unlocking it before handing it over, "Give me your phone then."

"Hey, a girl never gives away her secrets," she pulled up her contacts and handed her phone to him.

"You work in the fire brigade. Do you have any secrets?" He asked, with his head down typing.

Wouldn't you like to know? Handing back his phone, she murmured, "I still have a few. "

"I like a challenge." A loud clap of thunder echoed in the hills drowning out his chuckle.

A sheet of lightning arced overhead and the odd raindrop hit her face, "We should get undercover," she replied, grabbing her water bottle as they ran towards the tents. The rain got heavier as they got to the carpark. Reaching the tents, Blake paused pulling her wet shirt off her stomach. *I need some dry clothes for bed.*

Curled up in her sleeping bag, sleep wasn't an option with the constant noise of the rain on the roof, the tent wall flapping in the howling winds and the thunderclaps. *Based on the noise level inside the tent, someone is sleeping. Where are my earplugs?*

🚒 🚒

The following morning, the rain had washed the smoke from the blue sky. *The fires are out, thank God. Time to go home.* Blake grabbed her bag and headed out the door when Peter pulled her aside. With the two of them behind the tent, he gently rested his hand on her arm. Leaning in, he looked her straight in the eyes, "Are you going to be Okay?"

His closeness stirred something within. Feeling her face blush, she glanced back at her old crew making their way across the field. "Yes. The trip home will be better than the trip out," she tossed her bag over her shoulder, "I enjoyed working with your team."

"We enjoyed having you." He held his hand to say goodbye, "You know where to find us if you want a chat."

"Look forward to it," she replied with a friendly handshake.

"Are you coming?" Bo called out across the field.

"Yeah, I better find my crew," Peter replied, turning away he glanced back giving her a quick wave. Blake paused giving him a brief wave. Her eyes tracked him as he disappeared behind the tent. *I better hurry up.*

Scurrying over to the carpark, she stopped dead on the edge of the field. A layer of water sat between her and the truck. Tip-toeing through the mud in the roadside gutter, she placed her gear in the back compartment. Beside her the wheel ruts of another fire engine that had already left. The support crews had begun to dismantle the tent city. *I think the football team is going to want some work done.* She reached up and opened the back door, "Glad that is over."

"Not sitting in the front," Bo asked.

"Nope, Liam get in the front," she ordered stepping aside to let him pass. Numerous firefighters loaded their gear into their trucks as the engine pulled out of the carpark. She looked back at their faces as they passed by. *I don't recognise any of these guys.* Her thoughts returned to the first time Peter appeared from the smoke, just another stranger in the smoke and how he improved her week. *He is from my city and I don't remember him seeing him at any incidents.*

Bo pulled onto the highway followed by other trucks. With a two-hour trip ahead of her, Blake stretched out in the gap created by the missing crew member closing her eyes to grab a nap.

CHAPTER 5

BACK HOME

The weekend was over; Blake still had two more days of leave to recover from the wildfires. Her thoughts of the deployment rattled around her head as she shoved a load of washed clothes into the dryer. Stepping back she stumbled over the pile of dirty clothes still on the laundry floor. *One week so many clothes.* Checking her work pant pockets she pulled out handfuls of rubbish. Holding up a mint wrapper, brought back the memory of Peter's generosity. *Why did he come to me that day? It could have been anyone on the fire ground.*

Her gaze returned to the stains and mud coating her pants. *This needs a hot wash.* With the washing machine whirring away, she laid back on the couch, flicking through the TV channels. The apartment was too quiet after the chaotic week on the fire ground. Looking for something to do she turned her phone over. *No messages.* She stared up back at the screen. *What am I going to do for the next two days? What's on at the movies?* Flicking through the internet. *The latest Top Gun. Who am I going to invite to see it?* She flicked through her contacts, 'Peter Sycamore Awesome Day'. *Awesome? Really?* Her gaze lingered on the number. *Should I call him? What am I going to say? Nothing has happened since I got home.*

Slumping back on the couch. *He will be busy doing Captain stuff. Don't waste his time.* Sighing, she closed the screen. *I'll go to the movie by myself.*

Leaving the cinema, the neon bar sign caught her eye. *What the hell? A drink before I return to work.* The bar had the usual crowd, faces hidden in the shadows drowning their sorrows. Five men sitting in the corner brought back memories of the pub in Brook Hill.

Blake sat silent, taking a mouthful of beer when Trish slid across from her at the booth. "Since when did you drink beer?"

"I got to like it on deployment," Blake muttered.

"No vodka? That's a good sign. What happened?"

"I got swapped to another team," Blake looked down at her glass, "A good team. I met—" Pausing as her inner thoughts questioned where she stood with Peter.

"Met who?"

"No one. I have to get home and prepare for work tomorrow," she sculled the last mouthful of beer as she rose.

On her first day back at work after her break, Blake signed the time log. Something hit the floor in the storeroom, followed by some swearing. *What is that?* Curious about the racket, she stood in the doorway, Troy was back from his sick leave and busy checking the equipment. Bo focused on his laptop with his phone under his ear. The last of John's night crew walked out the door. And the radio had some chatter going on in the back corner. *Everything is back to normal.* She smiled as she placed her lunch in the fridge, closing the door the fire siren echoed through the garage. *Yep, back to boring city stuff. Now where's my fire jacket?*

🚒 🚒

Friday came around quickly. *Deployment, a week ago. It feels like yesterday.* Blake was filling out her travel forms when Bo placed a firehose nozzle on her desk. Raising her gaze to his face, "What am I doing with that?"

"Peter rang from Mansell Station; we acquired one of his nozzles last week. Drop it over to them when you're free."

They have only just noticed it's missing. Peter hasn't contacted me about it. Did they all take the week off? "Okay, I'll do it when I go to lunch."

Surrounded by traffic Blake sat at a stop light, resting a hand on the steering wheel and glanced at her phone. *Thirty minutes, this traffic is slow, I'll write this off as work and have a late lunch.* Pulled up at the front of Mansell station, she peered through the windscreen. *All the vehicles are here so someone should be in.* The garage was dark and empty except for two fire trucks waiting for their next mission. She stood outside Peter's office; he had his head buried in his work and didn't react to her presence. "Doesn't anyone work around here?" She called out with a grin.

Peter glanced up from his computer and gave her a wave to enter. Taking the nozzle from her hands, he headed for the garage, "Good to see you happier."

"Things have improved."

He laid the nozzle on the workbench. Glancing at the old wall clock ticking away, he asked, "Have you had lunch?"

"No, I'll get it on the way back."

Turning his head, he looked back curious, "Join me at the café?

Invitation to lunch. Her chest tightened and her pulse increased, "Café? Aren't you on call?"

"It's across the road, not the other side of town."

"Okay, sounds good."

He grabbed his phone from his desk before joining her at the front of the garage. Passing a crew member on the way out the door, Peter called back, "We will be across the road. Ring me if anything happens."

⬛ ⬛

We're lucky we got a table before the lunch crowd arrived. Blake silently looked over the rim of her coffee cup. Peter's bloodshot eyes from the fires had returned to white, bringing out their warm brown colour, and making him look friendlier. He glanced up from his burger and grinned as he reached for the sauce. *That fire T-shirt makes his shoulders pop. Away from work, he seems to have a softer side.*

"How was your break?" He asked.

"Housework and went to the movies."

Straightening his shoulders, he gave her his full attention, "Which movie?"

"Top Gun Mav—"

His wide eyes locked on hers, "You should have called me. I wanted to see that."

"Sorry, I didn't know. It was good."

"Don't tell me, I want to see it for myself," he replied taking a mouthful of soda.

So, he wanted me to call for the movie. "Have you been busy?" She asked.

"Yes and no. The usual. I'm looking forward to—" Peter's phone buzzed, glancing at the screen, he jumped to his feet rattling the table, "Fire. Got to go." He wrapped his half-eaten burger, in a napkin as he quickly asked, "Want to come fishing tomorrow?"

What? He's asking me fishing. She rose, her eyes connecting with his. "Fishing? For a first date?"

"If that's what you want," he replied with a smile, he looked back at the station. The phone buzzed one more time. He pulled Fifty dollars from his wallet and placed it in her hand, "For the bill. Call you later."

"No problem," her eyes followed him as he ran out the door. *I'm going to finish my burger first.* Retaking her seat, she stared out the window, watching him disappear into the garage. *Fishing? I better check my gear later.* Using her fingertips, she pulled the raw onion off her meat patty. *He didn't confirm or deny the date comment. Either way, it will be a good day out. Fishing with him, alone.* She smiled as a warm energy rose inside. The table vibrated as her phone rang. *Bo, is he checking up on me?*

"Where are you? We have fire on the north side." *Bo doesn't mess around with pleasantries.*

"I'm about to leave Mansell Station," her pulse increased as she stood up.

Bo mumbled to someone in the background before returning to her, "Get a lift with Peter, he has been called to it too. I'll grab your kit."

Flicking her gaze back at the station. *They're climbing in the truck. Oh, crap.* "Okay." She dropped the fifty-dollar note on the counter. "Keep the change," she called out as she bolted out the door.

Hurry up or you will miss them. Her pulse was racing as she waved trying to get Peter's attention. Darting through the traffic, she arrived at the truck as they closed the back door. "Room for one more?" She asked.

"Your gear?" Peter asked.

"Bo has it."

Squeezing in next to the guys, one asked, "Miss us?"

"Of course," she gripped the door handle as the siren rang out from the driveway. *Socialising is over, back to work. I didn't want lunch anyway.*

🚒 🚒

The house was well alight when Blake jumped out of Peter's truck and ran over to Bo to grab her kit bag. Her fears of the residents being trapped in the house were dismissed when she saw the owners standing on the footpath.

Flames leapt from the burning garage on the side of the house. The wailing sirens drew the attention of the street. A blue sedan roared up into the neighbour's driveway. The driver rushed over to the homeowner and started yelling. His face was getting redder as they both screamed at each other.

Blake threw on her helmet and rushed over to Bo, pointing back at the civilians fighting. His attention was drawn back to the house as the roof collapsed. Sparks and flames leapt into the air.

The neighbour rushed over to Peter and started yelling in his face. Peter stepped back as the resident joined the argument. The houseowner shoved the neighbour who returned with a fist which grew into a punch-up. Peter grabbed the neighbour's shoulder and pulled him away. He retaliated planting a fist to the side of Peter's head and pushing his face mask sideways. Grabbing the side of his face Peter stumbled backward. The neighbours went back to fighting each other.

Oh, crap. Peter! Blake ran over to him, her pulse increasing as she ran her eyes over his cheek, "A bit of a lump and no blood."

Another set of sirens entered the street as the police arrived. The sight of the officers made the fight fizzle back to a yelling match. Peter returned to the truck holding the side of his face.

🚒 🚒

Three hours later back at Mansell, hot and sweaty as usual. The crew had gone off to the showers. Blake draped her fire gear over the chair and turned to Peter, running her fingers near his sore cheek, "A small bruise," she moved closer, "Fishing, where are we going?"

He stepped aside and glanced out the window, "The weather is good. I'm thinking the reef."

The open sea. Raising her eyebrows, she smiled, "The reef, I don't get out there very often," stepping closer to him, "When and where should I me—" She paused as a crew member passed behind her. Her flushed cheeks were hidden behind her hot red face. Biting her lips to block her smile her eyes were fixed on Peter's face.

He stood silent, his eyes following the crew member into the kitchen before he looked back at her, "Call you later," he whispered with a straight face. "Thanks for dropping off the nozzle." His voice returned to normal as he turned towards the office.

Blake started to head for the exit when she spun around. *My gear.*

CHAPTER 6

FUN DAY FISHING

Later that evening Blake was buzzing with energy, excited about getting out on the water. "Fishing rod, tackle box. Now what to wear," Cranking the music up loud, she dug around in her wardrobe. Her eyes darted between the cargo pants on her old fishing outfit and her red bikini, "Fishing or date?" Her phone rang on her side table. *Peter.* The call started with clanging sounds coming from his end. *Has he accidentally dialled my number?* "Hello?"

"Crap. Hi. I just dropped the esky. I'm packing the boat."

"Okay. I can call you back later."

"No, it's good. I'll meet you at the marina in the morning. The boat trailer won't fit in your street."

"The marina. What time?"

Giving a few groans followed by more banging sounds, he replied, "High tide is just after dawn. How does six sound?"

Easing down onto her bed, "Good. What do you want me to bring?"

"Whatever you want. I have spare gear and food," he replied as something else crashed, "Heck. I'll see you in the morning."

"See you there." Hanging up the phone, she looked up with a smile. *With all that noise he planning something big. Maybe he should have rung me after he packed the boat.*

🚒 🚒

The first rays of the sun came over the hills. Blake leaned against the front of her car; a growing knot in her stomach had her nerves tingling. Focusing on the seagulls circling overhead, she tried to distract her thoughts. The marina was busy with SUVs and boats coming and going. *What car does he drive?* A car horn blasted nearby making her jump and look around. *It's not him.*

A lone figure headed towards her, their features hidden by the sun's rays behind him. *Peter? Is he already here?* Her pulse quickened as she stepped away from her car with a smile.

He is cheery for this hour of the morning. Standing before her, he reached out with a friendly hug. "You look good. I like red."

Blake glanced down at her long beach shirt, partly buttoned up over her red bikini underneath, "Thanks." Lifting her gaze to connect with his, she reached out her fingers, straightening his collar, "That colour suits you." *It brings out your eyes.* The pale blue shirt and reef shorts accented his toned, tanned legs.

"Ready to catch some dinner?" He asked.

"I didn't see you arrive?"

"I know, I waved and you ignored me," he bent over and picked up her fishing tackle box.

She strolled beside him towards the marina with her bag under one arm and her fishing rod in the other. "I've never seen your private vehicle. I'm used to seeing you in the fire fleet."

"The white Ranger over there," he replied, pointing to a distant vehicle and trailer.

The concrete steps led down to the timber marina decking. A gurgling sound came from the waves under the boards as she moved over the deeper water. The cool breeze and the smell of the sea added to her energy level from her breakfast coffee. Boats of various sizes and price tags lined the jetty. "Which one is yours?"

"This one." He replied, stepping onto a thirty-foot all-white deck.

Nice. Tall fishing rods stuck out above the driver's cabin. The words 'Awesome Day' were stretched along the side. *Awesome Day. Is that what he meant in my contacts? He has a motto.*

She paused and scanned the boat. *Wow. Look at the size of this thing. Twin motors and a large esky across the back. He likes fishing.* Stepping on board her eyes ran over the interior. White everywhere with thin strips of grey as a trim. *It's so clean.*

Peter took the fishing rod from her hand placing it in a holder "Stow your gear under the foredeck."

Under the foredeck? Pushing open the door next to the driver's console, revealed a low cabin naturally lit with two small portholes. A foam bed ran from one side of the hull to the other. Kitted out with fluffy pillows, a blanket and wall lighting. "It comes with a bedroom?"

"Yeah, handy for camping trips."

Camping too. I want to hang out with this guy more often. Pushing down on the mattress, her eyes slowly panned the room. *I could sleep here.* A dull rumble started as the motors engaged. *It is pretty quiet for so much horsepower.* Returning to the deck, she eased down into the passenger seat, her eyes scanning the console.

Glancing back towards him, questions ran through her mind. *Is this a date? What is he thinking?*

The early morning seas were calm as they left the bay. Out past the headland, the sunrise cast a golden glow on everything. Heading out to sea, the boat sliced through the waves. Blake wandered around the deck, peering over the side, the refreshing sea spray caught in the wind hitting her face. Her long brown hair danced in the breeze, circling across her vision. Flicking her hair aside, she noticed Peter looking back at her from the corner of his eye. Returning a smile, she moved undercover, gliding her hand across the back of the driver's seat. The smooth vinyl was still soft. She leaned over his shoulder, her cheek beside his, "Nice boat."

He looked back with a smile as he rose, "Take the wheel, keep her straight. I'll get us some drinks." With one hand on the wheel, he leaned back against the console.

Blake's chest tightened as she slowly eased past him to the seat. Face to face, her eyes fixed on his as she passed. His spicy cologne stood out against the sea air. The light touch of his arm hair brushing against her arm sent tingles through her body. Wanting to look back, she focused on the waters ahead. *Don't get too excited, it's just fishing.*

Peter handed her a lemon squash. The icy water dripped off the bottle and ran down her arm making her jump. "Thanks," she slipped the bottle into the cup holder and wiped her hand on her shirt. He grinned and leaned back in the passenger seat with his feet on the handrail.

He looks relaxed. "Do you want to drive?" She asked.

"Have you had enough?"

"No, I'm good." She sipped her drink, "How much further?"

"About half an hour. Just say when you have had enough." He flicked through his phone, turning on some music.

I like this song. "How often do you come out here?" She asked, her body swaying to the beat.

"I come out with crew about once a month."

Several creatures jumped out of the sparkling water ahead of the boat. Blake pulled back on the throttle, "The dolphins are having fun."

Peter stood up and looked over her shoulder, his facial stubble tickled her cheek. He reached forward, pointing to the fish finder screen, "They are chasing those small fish." With his hand on the back of the chair, he stood beside her, his gaze fixed on the fish finder as the boat bobbed along. After a short time, he tapped her shoulder, "Let me, I will find us some fish." He slid behind her as she rose, gently running his hand across her back as she stepped aside. Her pulse increased as she looked out the corner of her eye. *Stone-faced like nothing is happening. Subtle.*

🚌 🚌

The sun was overhead, Blake stood at the back of the boat looking out to sea when her fishing reel whirred and pulled tight, "Got one," she grunted. Heaving back and forth her arm fought the pull on the line. Flashes of silver rose to the surface of the waves and dipped again. Sweat beaded on her brow with each deep breath. *My abs, I don't need to do sit-ups today.*

Peter leaned over the side of the boat with his net. His biceps were pumping as he pulled the fish aboard. "Two and half feet. You have dinner for a week," he said dropping the fish on the deck.

Taking a deep breath, she wiped her brow on her sleeve, "I have some work to catch up to your four."

"I'm not greedy, we can share." He looked up from the deck, "Do you want a pic?"

Right.

It took two hands to hold up her catch. She adjusted her grip on the slippery scales. Looking back at Peter, she smiled as he took the photo. *Damn, this fish is heavy.* Her smile turned into a grimace as her burning arm muscles quivered. *I don't need the gym today.* Placing the fish back on the deck, she shook out her cramping hands.

He stepped alongside holding the screen in front of her. "That's good," she replied glancing back at him. Taking a step back she leaned her head over his shoulder, "Group pic," she smiled as he held up the camera.

He looked at the screen, "We can do better," he wrapped his arm around her and drew her closer. His smile beamed as the camera clicked. "One more." As the camera clicked, his soft lips gently pressed against her cheek. Her heart skipped a beat as her eyes widened. Pulling back he looked down at that photo, turning the phone towards her, "That's better."

Glancing up from the screen, her gaze lingered on his sparkling eyes. *He is serious.* She fought a coy smile as her cheeks blushed. Kneeling on the deck he handed the phone towards her. Pulling back she held up her palms, "I'm covered in fish."

"Oh, the basin is under the passenger seat," he replied, packing the fish in the ice box. Waiting beside the seat to wash his hands, "Want a swim?"

A swim would be good...but. Wiping her hands on her towel, "Do you want to get eaten by a shark?"

"Not here. There is a sheltered bay on an island about fifteen minutes away."

⛟ ⛟

The white sands stood out against the clear blue waters. Tall palms punched through the undergrowth. Blake scanned the area. "We are alone."

"Even better," he replied, pulling up near the shore. The waves gently rocked the boat as he dropped the anchor. "I can't get any closer, we will have to swim ashore."

Blake dug around in the bag pulling out a bottle of sunscreen. Slipping her shirt off, she tossed it on the seat. Stretching her leg out on the side of the boat, she slowly rubbed sunscreen over her body. Stepping towards Peter she held out the bottle, "Can you do my back?" Not saying anything his gaze fixed on hers as she turned around. She gasped as the cool lotion ran down her spine. The gentle touch of his hands slowly following the contours of her back gave her goosebumps. Her insides tingled as she closed her eyes.

His hands pulled away, "My turn."

She turned around, as he unbuttoned his shirt and slid it down his arm. Her heart skipped a beat, her eyes slowly rising over his abs ending at his cheery gaze. *Toned but overdone.* With a cheeky smirk, he turned around looking out to sea. The lotion made it easy for her hands to glide over his broad shoulders. Tenderly feeling each rippling muscle had her heart racing. He turned around coming face to face. Holding her breath, she stood still as his gaze was drawn to her face. *What's he doing?*

Reaching up, he ran his fingers lightly over the side of her nose, "Missed a bit." His gaze lingered before he stepped back, "Swim?"

Seeing him drop over the side, Blake took a deep breath. *He enjoyed that. I enjoyed that.* Taking hold of the railing, she slipped into the warm waves and looked back at Peter treading water beside her. *Let's have some fun.* Blake gave a cheeky smile, "The last one to shore has to buy the other a drink at the pub." With a deep breath, she took off swimming. Reaching the shore, she wiped the salt water from her eyes, spinning around to see Peter casually paddling towards her. "Are you even trying?" She asked.

"No, I was picturing our next date at the pub." He paused not far from shore and looked back at her. His head and square shoulders stood out above the waves. That cheeky smile and warm eyes called her. *He has a warm confidence—a stillness. All the fires, I haven't seen him lose control. Even when he was mad at Tim, he was controlled. He is just sitting there, not demanding anything but waiting for me to decide my next move. Those eyes give away the desires he is too polite to say. Oh, what the hell?*

She slipped back into the water, diving under an approaching wave. Rising not far from his body, she flicked her wet hair to the side. Her eyes connected with his as she moved closer, "You owe me a beer," she murmured.

"Dinner at the pub it is. Saturday."

Moving closer, she replied, "Sounds good."

"Are you enjoying your fishing?" He asked in a low voice, "I hope you are; I want to do this again."

She nodded with a beaming smile. *So, do I.* Those warm brown eyes drew her in. Every muscle tingled as she slowly moved closer. Blake stepped forward slowly sliding her hands around his chest and looked deeply into his eyes, "I so want to kiss you," she whispered.

He leaned forward, his dilated pupils slowly moving from her gaze to her soft lips and back. The gentle touch of his hand brushing her cheek made her pulse jump. Goosebumps rose over her body; her eyes closed as his warm lips tenderly met hers. As they parted, his fingers brushed her neck, his electric touch sent a shiver down her spine. Cradling her head in his hands he caressed her lips in a long, slow kiss.

Her embrace was firm as she drew him closer. With her fingers running through his hair, his lips turned salty as a large wave rained down over them both. She gasped as she wiped her hair from her face and said, "Let's go ashore."

Strolling along the beach, hand in hand, "Not a bad first date," Peter said.

"Is this a first date? What about the café and the evenings sitting in the dark on the field?"

"While enjoyable, not date worthy. I would have done it with anyone needing to talk," he paused, "And the café was a false start."

True. She dropped her head on his shoulder, taking hold of his arm, "This is a great first date."

They wandered along the high tide line with the afternoon sun warming their backs. Blake turned to face him, "Why did you approach me that day on the fire ground? You could have sent over any of your crew or ignored me."

"Your eyes connected with me after Tim yelled," his voice dipped, "I felt your pain."

Leaning closer, "Was that you?"

"Yep, your gaze told me you needed someone to talk to."

Can't keep secrets from him. She wrapped her arms around him, "I'm glad you did."

"Me too," he whispered, running his fingers through her hair as his lips caressed hers.

They kept wandering around the tide line. *Say it.* She leaned in closer, "I was certain, you would have a girlfriend."

"I have had a few women chase after me over the years but they were more interested in shopping than fishing," he draped his arm across her shoulder, "I meant what I said at the pizza night. I prefer a woman who wants fun, like fishing."

"I was too tired that night, to work out your cryptic messages."

"Noted." The stroll around the small island continued until they were back at the start looking at the boat. Sitting arm in arm on the high tide line, the waves lapped their feet. Peter leaned his head on hers as they watched the wildlife scamper along the sand. "You didn't call me when you got back," he said.

"What was I going to say? I didn't know you wanted me to call," She turned towards him. "Anyway, you didn't call me."

"I didn't know how you felt. You didn't react to my hint at our pizza dinner."

"Hint? I was half asleep."

He paused, "But you could have invited me to see Top Gun."

She looked back at him, "We were together for four days and we didn't work that bit out."

"We were busy being firefighters." He pushed her hair behind her ear, moving his face closer to hers. "Sorry, I didn't call. Do you want to go out again?"

What? Leaning in with a kiss, she grinned, "With lunch next time."

He pulled back, "Oh, that's on the boat. I am getting hungry too."

They both sat on the side of the boat in the sun, finishing their salad rolls. Blake pushed aside her hair fluttering in the wind and adjusted her bikini strap, "We have probably washed our sunscreen off."

"Yeah, you don't want to burn."

She glanced back at him raising an eyebrow, "You weren't going to knock back that opportunity again," she rose to grab her bag.

"Didn't hear you complaining," he called out.

Returning to his side, she dug around in the bag, taking hold of her phone as she searched for the sunscreen.

"Want to show off to your girlfriends? Get a pic with a bare-chested Firey," he chuckled.

Oh, Geez. He wants to show off, not as self-conscious as I thought. "You show these pics to anyone at work and I will throw you overboard," she replied.

"Noted."

She leaned in, her cheek against his, holding her phone at arm's length. The photo of them laughing with his bare shoulders and her red bikini against the blue waves in the background summed up the day. "One more for us," she said, her lips met his as the camera clicked.

Peter looked back at the pics of the day, "Send me a copy," he paused as he went to hand back her phone, "Bugger, it's two o'clock, we should head back. We have to clean those fish."

The motors started up; Peter was in the driver's seat heading for the coast. Blake slipped her shirt back on and stood between the two seats. Peter glanced over his shoulder, tapping his thigh, "Have a seat if you want."

On his leg? Sitting on his thigh didn't provide a lot of padding on the bumpy waves. Peter wrapped one arm around her waist and controlled the boat with the other. Blake draped her arm across his shoulders to steady herself. Her fingers casually ran through his hair. The saltwater left it not as soft as she remembered. Accidentally brushing the side of his neck sent a shiver down his back. It didn't take long for him to reduce the motor speed back to idle.

"What's up?" She asked.

Looking back at her face, he slid his other arm around her waist. "It is difficult to focus with the distractions."

"Oh, sorry," she went to stand when he gently pulled her back.

"No, I like it but we should postpone it until later tonight."

Tonight? Her insides churned. Draping her arms over his shoulders. "What's happening tonight?"

"I don't know. You should come to my place and clean the fish," he replied with a beaming smile.

"Clean the fish?" She rose, "Sounds good. Do you want a drink from the Esky?"

"Thanks." The motors fired up once more.

CHAPTER 7

THE SECRET IS OUT

The glare of the sun low on the horizon blinded Blake as she pulled into Peter's driveway. It took a moment for her eyes to refocus. *Wow, that house is too big for one person.* The two-storey brick building overshadowed the white hull and ranger below. Peter poked his head over the side of the boat, "Hey, just unpacking."

He is still in his fishing clothes. I don't think he has had a shower yet. Climbing down the back of the boat, he still had the energy to greet her with a warm hug and kiss.

"Grab the other side of the Esky," he said taking hold of the handle. Labouring under the weight of the fish, they made their way to his backyard. The gateway opened up to a large expanse of lawn with a few trees along the back fence. A long table sat near the veranda ready for the task ahead. "Hope they are your dirty clothes," he said pulling a fish off the ice.

With the fish scaled, cleaned up and bagged away in the freezer, Peter washed the outdoor table with the hose. Blake held out her fishy hands and said, "I need another shower."

His eyes rose to meet hers, his dimples accented his cheeky grin. "You asked for it."

Anticipating his move, she turned away from him, shielding her face. The cold water spray ran down her back and made her gasp. *Not the first hose a firefighter has turned on me. I can play this game.* She lunged forward grabbed his hand and turned the spray back onto him. The hand-in-hand tussle and laughing went on for a short while until they were both soaked. The hose-down did not put out their fire. Looking deep into her soul, the hose hit the pavement as he drew her body against his, embracing her with a loving kiss.

The cool night air and her wet clothing sent a shiver over her body. "Do you have a towel," she asked. She sat on the back veranda dripping water when Peter handed her one of his old towels. The outdoor lounge, barbeque and dinner setting made her want to stay longer. *Set up for some interesting parties.* Peter stood in the laundry doorway and asked, "Want to stay for dinner?"

Tempting but I'm getting tired. "Thanks, but I need to head home for another shower," she paused, "A hot one."

Strolling down the driveway, he leaned over with a kiss goodbye, "Call you later." She went to hand him his towel, "Keep it for your car seat."

🚒 🚒

The following week, Blake lay across the fire truck seat, vacuuming the gravel off the floor. Her thoughts were elsewhere, going over how her life had changed since the deployment.

Another crew member sat in the front seat cleaning the windows. "How much did you pay Clyde to change teams?"

Where did that come from? Blake looked back from under her brow, "What are you talking about?"

"Did you find a better option to working with Tim?" His gaze fixed out the windscreen, "Maybe a captain to sink your teeth into."

Tension grew in her shoulders, "Shut up and get back to work," she ordered returning her focus to the floor. *Hasn't he got something better to do than ship me?*

Having finished one side of the floor, Blake shuffled along the bench, when a head appeared through the open door. A face only inches away filled her view. Her heart skipped a beat as she flinched, "Crap. Peter, what are you doing here?"

He held up her fishing tackle box and looked back with a cheeky smile, "You left it on my boat."

Bugger. And you had to bring it here. She glanced across to the crew in the front, the smirk on his face said he knew too much. *That explains the questions. He saw Peter in the garage.* "Go check the tyres," she ordered.

Climbing out of the truck, she leaned toward Peter and whispered, "You could have given it to me later." *Instead of advertising our fishing trip to the whole station.*

"Yeah, right when I pick up for the movie," he replied with a sparkle in his eye.

Raising an eyebrow, she muttered, "What movie?" *I don't remember anything about going to the movies. I'm sure he makes stuff up as he goes.*

"The one I bought tickets for tonight."

She turned her back to the crew and whispered, "What if I had other plans for tonight?"

"Repotting your dead plant," Peter's chuckle rang out through the garage.

Smart ass. I threw that out last week. Keeping a straight face, she focused on hiding her feelings from the crew by playfully thumping his chest, "Go check a fire hydrant."

"Hey, don't make me separate you two," Bo called out with a grin, "The last bloke she hit here, left me dealing with the complaint."

Blake glanced back at Peter taking the tackle box from his hand, "Thanks, call me when you leave work."

🚒 🚒

Later that night, on the drive back to Blake's home. "Top Gun Maverick. Why didn't you pick a different movie?" She asked adjusting the air vent to redirect the cold air off her arms.

"I wanted to see it."

"Well, it was still good the second time around."

"You should have invited me the first time," Peter casually replied. Waiting at the traffic lights, he took hold of her hand, "I'm fishing with the crew in three weeks. Do you want to come?"

With the crew, our secret won't last long now. A lump grew in her throat. She glanced back nervous, "Fishing with five blokes on that boat. A bit cramped."

"No, they are going out on Ted's boat." Peter's voice softened, "We will have the boat to ourselves."

Oh, to ourselves. "Sounds good."

"We are camping out at an island group for the night. Make a full weekend of it."

Camping on an island. That thought raised her excitement briefly but then a vision of the crew sitting across from her killed those feelings. "A weekend with the whole crew." She replied hesitantly. *I have to control myself for the whole weekend with him. Oh, what the hell, they have shipped us already. I have seen how both crews look at us.*

"What is the problem? You spent four whole days with them," he replied slowing for a roaming dog on the road, "I'll be there to protect you."

"I don't need protecting." She paused, "I will have to threaten to throw them overboard too."

"Noted," he replied pulling up in front of her home.

She turned toward him, her hair falling over her shoulder, "Do you want a coffee?"

"No, I have an early start." Leaning over with a tender kiss, "Talk tomorrow."

Standing on the top step, she waved as he pulled back into the traffic. Heading for the elevator, the thought of a weekend camping with his crew played in her mind. She took a long, slow breath to calm her nerves and hit the fifth-floor button. *I have to replace my worn-out sleeping bag. Are we camping on the beach or on the boat? I will have to write down these questions.*

CHAPTER 8

BAD NEWS

A few days later. "Charged, all clear," Blake called out with a defibrillator paddle in each hand.

"Clear," Troy replied.

The concrete floor made her knees ache. She reached across the first aid mannequin when someone came into her peripheral vision. "That will have to wait," Bo said standing beside her.

Glancing over her shoulder, a woman dressed in a suit stood beside him. *Who is she?* "What's up?"

"In my office," Bo replied in a flat tone.

Discharging the paddles she handed them to Troy. She wiped her brow on her shirt, "Can I get a drink first?"

"Sure."

Blake cautiously entered Bo's office; he quietly closed the door behind her. The unknown woman sat at the desk in Bo's seat. *Is this our new boss? Has Bo finally been promoted?*

Standing against the wall, Blake tried to read the room. Bo wasn't giving away anything and the woman's cold expression created an unease. Her short-cropped hair and lack of makeup added to her unfriendly persona. *I hope she is not our new boss.* Blake turned towards Bo, "What is going on?"

"This is Vicki Wade from Human Resources," He replied as he sat in the corner.

Why is HR here? Blake looked back confused, opening her mouth but not knowing what to say. Her chest tightened. *What is going on?*

"Take a seat. I'm here to investigate your incident with Tim Smythe in the garage. Where you hit him."

Hit him? Oh. Blake dropped down in the seat next to the desk and took a long breath. Her eyes darted from the pile of paperwork to Vicki's scour. *Tim is still causing problems. Goodbye, promotion.* Blake's shoulders slumped as she looked away.

"I have read Captain Bosham's report—a lot of reading for a single incident," Vicki held up a handful of papers.

"What do you want from me?" Blake asked, shuffling in her seat.

"Mr Smythe has put in a formal complaint about your assault."

"Assault!" Blake sat bolt upright, her pulse racing. A heat rose in her face, her wide eyes locking with Vicki's cold gaze. *I should have left him on the fire ground.* Blake restrained her anger to her white knuckles gripping the chair armrests, "He started it." She turned back to Bo, her eyes wide before looking back to Vicki, "What about all the others he fought with? The chopper pilot, the police."

Vicki held up her palm blocking Blake's communication, "I have read all the reports. But it's formal, so you have to attend a mediation meeting next week."

"Mediation?" Blake replied and took a deep breath. "He better not be there," she fidgeted with agitation. Beads of sweat formed on her brow as her palms became clammy.

"Yes, he will be in another room," Vicki closed her folder, "I will email you the details in the next few days."

Blake lunged forward, "But. He caused that argument. How many of his insults and sexist slurs was I meant to take?"

Vicki rose, "That will do for now. I need to talk to Captain Bosham alone."

Don't I get a say? The chair rattled across the tile floor as Blake rose. *I can't believe this crap.* Bo stood behind the open door; his gaze briefly connected with hers. That look said he was as disappointed in the system as she was. Blake clenched her jaw; tension gripped her shoulders as she left the room. The door closed behind her as soon as she was clear.

Assault, I'll give him assault. Muttering to herself she hurried into the locker room. "Argh!" she cried out as her anger boiled over. The side of her fist hit the locker door making it fly open. Looking down at her kit. *I'm not sticking around to be called back in there.* Grabbing her bag and her car keys, she stormed into the garage.

"What's happening?" Troy asked, still doing CPR on the floor. Blake strode straight past him and said nothing. "Where are you going?"

Anywhere but here. She kept walking and didn't reply.

🚒 🚒

Speeding into the Mansell station driveway, one truck was missing. *He better be here.* The traffic didn't help calm her anger. Blake strode into the station, not paying attention to anything in the garage.

Turning the corner toward Peter's office, she froze, her eyes widened. *What the?* He was looking at his laptop. A woman was standing behind him. Her hand on the back of his chair, she was leaning over his shoulder and looking at the screen. Under the guise of talking, she would have suffocated him if she had shoved her oversized chest any closer to his face. *Who is she?* Blake's teary eyes stared back as they both looked up from the computer. Peter's gaze connected with hers as she spun around and took off for her car. Unable to control her mixed emotions, her chest tightened, her world closing in around her as she slammed the car door. Tears flowed down her cheeks as she dropped her forehead on the steering wheel. *I thought he was better than that.*

A repeated knocking on her side window drew her attention. Peter peered back through the glass. "What's up?" He pulled on the door handle, "The door is locked."

She looked back with cold contempt. Starting her car, the engine reeved as she reversed into the traffic and sped towards the city.

🚒 🚒

Peter jumped back as Blake threw the car in reverse, pulling out of the driveway. *What is wrong with her?* He spun around to track her as she sped off into the traffic. *Slow down before you kill yourself.* Running back into his office he grabbed his phone and car keys. Jumping into the work four-wheel drive, he headed off in her direction. *Where is she going?* He scanned ahead trying to find her silver sedan in a sea of cars. Several blocks further, he pulled up at a traffic light. *Is that her?* He strained to see her number plate. Seeing a Fire brigade support sticker on the back window confirmed it was her. She was two cars ahead in the next lane. The heavy traffic had slowed her down, it took another block for him to merge in behind her.

I don't think she knows where she is going. After following her for three blocks, she turned into an off-street carpark. *Has she calmed down?* He pulled up beside her, she sat staring out the windscreen as he approached. Looking in the passenger window, "Blake, let me in. We need to talk." With no reaction, she kept looking ahead. Peter tried the door handle one more time. "Blake, open the door," he dropped his voice, "Please."

Without saying anything she pressed a button on her door panel, unlocking the passenger door.

Cautiously he climbed aboard and tried to make eye contact but she stared ahead. "Talk to me," he reached out taking hold of her hand. Tears flowed down her red cheeks.

Blake whipped her hand back, "Who is she?" Her words were laced with bitterness.

She? His blank expression lasted a few seconds before his eyes widened. "Who Gail? She was organising a time for our first aid training."

Blake turned her head, her bloodshot eyes full of tears rose to meet his, "Training?" She replied sounding less than convinced.

"Yes, she is a regular contractor."

"Bull. No one can do CPR with that chest."

What? "I've never noticed."

Her eyes widened, "Don't give me that crap! I'm not an idiot," she snapped back shaking her head as she looked away.

Boy, something has her fired up. Peter turned his body to face her in the cramped cabin, his gaze searching for answers, "What the hell has happened? You didn't get this upset over her chest."

Blake sat silent, taking several deep breaths. In the privacy of her vehicle, she spoke about the complaint and future hearing. Closing her eyes as she dropped her face toward the floor, tears ran down her cheek, "He is ruining it all for me. All my hard work was for nothing."

Oh crap. Assault. We have to talk. He took hold of her hand, placing the other on her shoulder. "It will be all right. Let's get some lunch and talk." Peering out the side window he scanned the surrounding businesses, spotting a small takeaway shop. *That's better than nothing.*

Blake waited in the car as Peter went to get their order. On his return they wandered over to a table in the local garden they sat across from each other. The park was quiet for that hour of the morning. Blake's anger had subsided but she wasn't in a chatty mood. She stared into the distance as she took a bite of her chicken roll. *What is she thinking about now?* He calmly grabbed one of her chips and dipped it in his sauce. "Ready for tonight?"

She looked back confused, "What?" She mumbled while swallowing and reaching for her drink.

"I remember you wanted to go to the pub for dinner."

Putting down her roll, she raised her eyebrows and tilted her head to the side, "I did?"

He leaned over wiping some sauce off the corner of her mouth with his thumb, "No, but you need cheering up."

"But what am I going to do with this hearing?" Her hand started to shake again as tears filled her eyes.

Chill woman. He gripped her hands, holding them still, "Get some character references from the crews you have worked with before." His eyes looked deep into hers, his voice softening, "And most important, be your cheerful self." He leaned over placing his sticky fingers under her jaw drawing her closer as his lips met hers. The burn of her chilli sauce made his lips tingle. *Argh, why did I choose a Mexican takeaway?*

Her pocket buzzed, and she glanced at the screen. "Bo, he is probably checking up on me."

"See, they care for you," Peter replied, taking a mouthful of soda to water down the chilli now burning the tip of his tongue.

She put the call on speaker mode and held it over the table. They both leaned over to hear the message.

"Where are you?"

"Having lunch with Peter."

"It's a quarter to eleven. Anyway, just seeing if you were all right."

"Never better." She replied in a flat tone, "I'll be back there soon." Ending the call, she slipped her back into her pocket. "We should get back to work."

Sculling the last of her drink, she grabbed her lunch as they returned to the vehicles. Peter stood beside her as she opened her door, "Call me if you have to assault anyone else."

"Are going to take the hit for them?"

He smiled, "Dinner. Seven at my place."

🚌 🚌

One last spray of cologne as a car pulled up out front. Peter grabbed his keys, opening the door as Blake reached the bottom step. Pausing, he gasped, his gaze ran down her figure-hugging black evening dress. A change from chunky boots, cargo pants and her dark fire T-shirt. *Her hair is draped over her shoulders just the way I like it.*

"Wow," he smiled, meeting her with a warm hug and kiss. *She smells good too. Her mood has improved from earlier.* Before closing the door, he reached to a side table and whipped out a red rose. Holding it before her made her cheeks blush and resulted in another kiss.

Buckled up he glanced back and asked, "How was your afternoon? No assaults?"

"Just a false alarm, that evacuated a full shopping centre."

Yeah, I hate those false alarms. He nodded and rested his hand on her arm, "I will get a new first aid contractor. Some old bloke."

"Don't spoil it for the blokes," she smiled, leaned forward coming face to face and whispered, "Just keep her chest out of your face."

"Noted, boss," he whispered back, moving closer with a loving kiss. "Now let's get some dinner, I'm starving."

CHAPTER 9

TENSION RELEASE

Blake's insides churned thinking about the meeting. Her pulse pounded as she climbed the wide staircase to the head office entrance. Pausing she glanced back over her shoulder to Peter sitting in his car. After checking in an administration worker escorted Blake into a back room to wait for the mediation hearing.

Placing her briefcase on the floor, her nerves had her body tingling. She scanned the room; the interior décor was simple. A counselling helpline poster hung on one wall. *Counselling is that for now or afterwards. Where's the TV?* A couple of torn magazines lay scattered on the side table. *Are they having budget cuts?* Pulling out her phone, she checked her emails.

The small back room had no windows and was getting stuffy. Blake shuffled in the lounge chair. Pulling on her tie, she loosened her collar. Unbuttoning her formal fire jacket, and waving the lapel did little to make her cooler. Glancing at her phone, she sighed. *Two hours. They said it would be about an hour. I haven't seen the mediator yet. What is going on next door?*

Her phone buzzed, *Text from Peter.* "How's it going?"

"Hasn't started yet." Slipping her phone back into her pocket, she looked down at the three tattered magazines once more. Picking up the magazine she had just read, she flicked through the pages. *I'm meant to be on duty. I told Bo I was going to be an hour. He will be looking for me. I should have taken the day off.*

The thud of a door closing next door rattled the wall. Her pulse increased as she lowered the magazine back on the table. *Here we go.* Footsteps grew louder as the door opened.

"Miss Davies, you can come in now," a different administration staffer said.

The meeting room was as bland and stuffy as the waiting room. A long desk surrounded by a handful of chairs overlooked a large TV in the corner. Shuffling to straighten her tie, she eased down in the seat as directed by the admin. The mediator entered through a side door taking a seat without saying a word. A secretary taking notes sat at the end of the desk looking as happy as the mediator. *Wow, I wouldn't want to work here.* The table was covered in paperwork; one pile was recognisable as the references and statements Blake had collected from her and Peter's crew. Being her first hearing, she sat silent; hesitantly looking back at the mediator. Her flushed face, stiff shoulders, and sour look did not improve Blake's confidence. The mediator didn't make eye contact as she flicked through the paperwork and scribbled away with her pen. *This doesn't look good.* Blake re-adjusted her tie; her clenched palms became clammy.

Shuffling papers, the mediate twisted her neck side to side, she glanced up briefly before she looked back at her notes, "Miss Davies, having reviewed all the documentation and spent far too long talking with Mr Smythe. I have determined, that he was the cause of your retaliation. My recommendation is that the whole fire department undergo HR training in various subjects including sexism and bullying. As Mr Smythe no longer works in the department, I will close this case with no further action needed." She looked up for the first time during the speech, "In future, if anyone acts similarly, walk away and contact your HR rep."

Blake looked back blankly, "Okay." *All this stuffing around for a two-minute speech. And I still didn't get to say anything. I didn't need to be here. A week of crap for nothing.* Her pent-up frustration over the last month rose to the surface. Clenching her jaw to stay professional, she sat quietly as the mediator stacked the paperwork into bigger piles.

The mediator rose from her chair, "We are running behind time. You can leave now."

No pleasantries, just leave. What the? Blake grabbed her briefcase and headed straight for the entrance, unbuttoning her jacket as she went. Her anger grew with each step. *If he has stuffed up my promotion, he better never have a house fire.* She glanced sideways at Bo sitting in the foyer as she stormed out the door. Scampering down the stairs to Peter waiting in his car.

Peter bent over the passenger seat and opened the door, barely having time to sit back up as Blake jumped in the seat. Clipping up her seat belt, she ripped her tie from her neck. Her furrowed brow and clenched jaw showed her mood. "How did it go?" Peter calmly asked.

"I sat in a back room all morning, while she fought with Tim next door. I saw her for a few minutes, only to be told, the case was closed, no action required." Blake stared ahead, kicking her briefcase aside as she straightened her legs.

"No action. That's good," he sounded relieved placing his hand on her arm.

"And the whole department has to undergo HR training," she added in a flat tone.

"Oh fun. So, where do you want to go?"

"Fishing," she snapped back. *Get me away from this crap.* Her phone buzzed, "Bo, I don't want to talk to anyone."

Peter held out his hand, "Do you want me to talk to him."

"Whatever excites you," she replied, handing over her phone.

Holding the phone to his ear, Peter looked back, nodding. "A good as expected," he paused, "Okay, we are going fishing this afternoon," he said before nodding some more. "Sure, bye." Handing back her phone, he prepared to drive off.

"What did he say," she asked.

"Just seeing how you were going. And he has approved your afternoon off to attend counselling."

What the? No, bloody way, I'm going fishing. She flicked her head towards Peter. "Counselling?"

"Counselling, fishing, same thing," he smiled as he headed for her home.

Oh. Her shoulders dropped as she took a deep breath. Dipping her head, she closed her eyes. *Got to use the right words to fill in the reports. I need a lot more counselling with Peter.*

A hand touched her shoulder, "Hey, it's over. Smile."

He's right, it is over. Why didn't I find this guy earlier? She turned her head towards him taking hold of his hand and forced a tired smile.

Pulling up in front of her home, he leaned over, "Are you going to be Okay?"

"Yeah."

"See you at the marina in an hour."

She reached over, grabbing his arm, "No, wait here, I'll be a minute."

The car door closed and he leaned out the window as she crossed the street, "Blake, bring your overnight bag, it is getting late."

🚌 🚌

The calm sea breeze added to the peace of being alone on the reef. Blake didn't break a sweat reeling in her second fish. *It is just over a foot long, and not picture-worthy.* Opening the esky the three other fish didn't take up much room. *That won't feed us for long but we have only been out here for two hours.* She rinsed her hands as Peter reeled in another fish. *He has to beat me again. Look at the size of that, not even a meal.* He removed the hook and released the under-sized fish back into the waves.

The golden hues of the setting sun reflected off the waves. Having relaxed from a stressful morning, her limbs hung heavy. "I think that's enough fishing for today," Blake said, grabbing a drink from the cooler.

Peter paused as he reached for the bait bucket, "Do you want to head home?"

Home or an island? Visions of a hot shower and soft bed were tempting. *But an island is away from everyone.* She looked back with a blank expression. *If I go home, we can enjoy the luxuries in comfort.* She stepped forward wrapping her arms over his shoulders, "Home, a hot shower and a massage sounds great."

He raised his eyebrows as his face lit up, "Good idea."

The mainland grew on the horizon, Blake was in the driver's seat. Peter stood behind her and slowly massaged her shoulders. His gentle touch was a mixture of relief and confirmation of her aching muscles. She slowed the motors as she reached the bay giving the controls to Peter to load the boat on the trailer.

Driving back through the traffic in the dark Blake leaned against the door silent. The day of stress and ocean air had drained her energy.

🚌 🚌

Back at Peter's place, he grabbed the esky of fish and dropped it in the corner of the laundry. "They are in enough ice to last till morning."

He grabbed a fresh towel from the linen cupboard, "I'll have a shower before I order dinner."

"Okay, I'll call a taxi, thanks for taking me fishing," she leaned over for a good night kiss.

"No, stay for dinner."

Stay? The stress of the morning rose to the surface. Pausing, she looked back at him standing in the hall. Stepping forward, she slid her arms around his waist, "I don't want to be alone tonight. Can I stay the night?"

"Anytime," he pushed aside her wind-blown hair. "I look forward to your company." His deep gaze drew her focus, after a moment of silence, he stepped back, "Shower. You're distracting me again."

Taking a deep breath, her gaze tracked him down the hall. Digging around in her backpack; she pulled out a damp towel. *Damn, I wasn't planning on having a shower out of the reef tonight.* Holding up a shirt. *If I wear this now, what will I wear home tomorrow? A bikini? Should I drop past home and get some clothes?*

The shower went silent, followed shortly after by Peter wandering to his bedroom wrapped in a bathrobe. "Do you have a spare towel?" She called out down the hall. He returned with a towel and a dark blue fluffy bathrobe.

Refreshed from the steaming shower, she slipped on his bathrobe. The shoulder seams hung halfway down her biceps and the sleeves over her hands. Looking down at the hem, it came halfway down her shins. *Not quite my size.* She rolled up the sleeves and wrapped her hair in the towel as she walked towards the kitchen.

Peter came out of the laundry with a basket of clothes. His eyes started at the floor, rising towards her face. "Looks good," he chuckled with a cheeky grin.

Sitting at the table, she wiped her hair, "What's the plan for dinner?"

"I have ordered some pizzas." He aired confidence, wandering around in front of her in nothing but a bathrobe. Casually removing two glasses from the cupboard, he had no interest in getting dressed any further.

"I should drop home and get some clothes," she replied, pulling up her sleeve.

Peter returned to his bedroom, reappearing moments later, he gently tossed her one of his white button-up office shirts. "Dinner wouldn't be far off," he said as he opened the fridge.

Holding up the shirt, the scallop hem came just above her knee. *I have dresses shorter than this.* Looking down at the robe hanging from her body. *Well, it's smaller than this tent.* Back in the bathroom, she finished buttoning up the shirt and rolled up the sleeves. Running her hand up her arm, the pure cotton fabric was thick and soft. *Nice.*

"Dinner," his deep voice boomed through the wall.

Pulling the towel from her hair she tossed it in the hamper as she left the bathroom. The dining table was empty. *Where did he go?* She peered out the front window, nothing but darkness. A voice came from the kitchen, "Do you want red or white?"

Red? Oh, wine. "White. Where's dinner?"

"In the cinema room, let's chill with a movie."

🚌 🚌

The empty pizza boxes sat on the side table. Peter stretchered out on the luxurious lounge, tucking a fluffy pillow under his shoulder. Blake nestled back against his chest, sipping her wine. As the movie started, Peter pressed the remote, and the overhead lights faded to black. His hand softly returned to her shoulder.

The room air conditioner was colder than she liked, but this gave her reason to snuggle closer to his warm body. His fresh clean smell was a refreshing change from the manly sweat odour she experienced at work. As the evening went on, she pulled the blanket over her legs. He wrapped his arm around her shoulder drawing her closer in a warm embrace.

Sitting silently watching the movie, Blake's arm draped over his waist and rested on his opposite hand. Her attention was drawn away from the movie; she stared at his manly hands. Slowly running her fingers over the soft hairs on his forearm, her thoughts turned inward. She raised her head, whispering in his ear. His eyes darted from the screen and locked with hers. *That got your attention.* A fire grew inside her as his hand brushed her cheek, his soft lips caressing hers as their passion rose. Her heart rate increased as her fingers fiddled to untie the knot on his robe. They lost all interest in the movie.

CHAPTER 10

ISLAND CAMPING

The three weeks came around fast. Up before dawn, Blake parked in front of Peter's house. A nearby street light reflected off the white hull. The words 'Awesome Day' stood out the most. Peter had been up and busy for a while, the car and boat were packed ready to go in the driveway. He tossed his bag on his back seat as she walked up the driveway. His cheery face and warm hug made up for getting up early. *Look at all that stuff. He must have big plans.* Two yellow sea canoes were tied to side rails.

He slipped her bag from her shoulder, "What no bikini?"

Is that how you greet someone? "I'm not wearing that with the whole crew."

He shrugged his shoulders, "Okay. Next time," he placed her bag next to his and opened the passenger door, "Are you ready for a busy weekend?"

"You have certainly packed for one."

"We don't do things by halves," he closed the passenger door after she climbed inside.

He is a gentleman. Her gaze followed him as he scurried around the front of the car, jumping into the driver's seat.

Heading out of town, the traffic was light for that hour of the morning. Blake looked up from her phone, the open highway ahead was lined with bushland. "Where are we going?" She asked.

"A jetty further up the coast. It is closer to the islands we camp at," He handed her a travel cup, "Ted is meeting us there."

Taking hold of the cup, she raised an eyebrow, "What's this?"

"Coffee, same as you ordered at the café."

He makes café coffee? "Thanks, I had coffee before I left." She cautiously took a sip to test the temperature. *Nice.*

"You need your energy if you want to beat us at fishing," he chuckled.

Five blokes, fishing. "I might stay out of that competition."

"That's not the firefighter I have seen. You run with the best of them," he checked the mirrors before changing lanes. "You're scared we will catch more than you?"

"You want to start a fight—" Her phone buzzed. *A text from Bo, he better not be calling me back to work.* Opening the message, her eyes widened as she lowered the phone to her lap, "Oh crap."

"What?" Peter asked glancing back over his shoulder.

"Bo is going on holiday and I have been nominated to fill his role."

Peter's face lit up as he held up his hand for a high five, "Good on you. Acting Captain Davis."

His cheery voice was a bit much for that hour of the morning after receiving such news. Half-heartedly slapping his hand, she mumbled, "Don't get too excited, it's just two weeks."

"Practice for your promotion."

"Or an assessment."

"Hey, you'll do just fine. If you get stuck, ring me. And you have Captain John at the Station."

"He gets grumpy if you ring him after hours. People don't ring him."

"You have my number," Peter replied, changing lanes to pass an old van.

🚃 🚃

The old timber jetty was vaguely visible through the first rays of sunshine. To the right of the peer, sat a wide concrete boat ramp running back into the waves. *Ted is already unloading his boat.* A twenty-foot grey aluminium hull with a fold-back canopy shading the stand-up console. *It's not as big as this one.* "Four of them in that? It's not that big." Blake said wandering down to the ramp.

"Only three today, Alex had other plans." Peter replied while untying his hold-down straps, "What did you expect on his pay? It took me years of captain's pay to save up for this boat."

Without the protection of the bay, the choppy water at the jetty made climbing aboard an exercise in coordination. With everything finally loaded, Peter headed out to sea with Ted following.

About an hour later, Blake faced the sun, taking long slow breaths and enjoying the warm sea breeze. Flicking her hair down-wind, she scanned this unknown part of the coast. The crew in the second boat were further out. A larger island with smaller islands nearby appeared on the horizon. The song on Peter's phone had her body swaying as she came to sit down, "Which Island are we camping at?"

"That one," he replied pointing to the largest island in the group. "But first we are fishing over there," pointing to a patch of ocean with a few birds diving into the waves.

Anchored near the reef, the day was busy with fishing, the esky cooler was getting full. Blake tossed another fish on the ice, "That's four for me, it's a tie."

"Eight. We have ten," Ted yelled from the other boat.

"There's three of you. So, we are in front," Blake called back with a cheeky smile.

Peter handed her a cold drink, "Don't go upsetting my crew."

"Put in a formal complaint to head office."

He dropped in the driver's seat, pressing buttons to start the outboard motors, "It's not worth the paperwork." Looking over his shoulder at the motors, he replied, "I'll deal with you later."

Later? She eased into the passenger seat and glanced back, "Oh, really. And how are you going to do that?"

"Stop distracting me," he replied as they moved to a different part of the reef.

After catching a couple more fish, everything started to take on a golden glow as the sun sat above the horizon. They anchored off the main island for the night. A sandy beaches circled a forest of palms, rocky slopes and undergrowth. Peter loaded the canoe with the food esky before paddling ashore.

Very little paddling was required from Blake as she rode a wave into the beach. *Saves me swimming this time.*

The crew set up a crude tent at the top of the beach. Peter and Blake set out along the high tide line gathering driftwood for the fire. "Where are we camping?" She asked.

"The boat is ready to go. I'm over tents," Peter replied as he wandered up the beach into the setting sun.

In the next bay, and with the crew out of sight, Blake piled her wood on a large rock. Sliding her hands behind his back, "I'm going to have to control myself this weekend with the boys here."

"They know what is going on," he drew her closer, "Just chill."

"Did you tell them?"

"No, but why else would I invite you fishing with them? They are not idiots."

Resting her head on his chest, "Okay. You know them best."

He pulled back, "While we're here," he slid his hand behind her head, leaning in with a loving kiss.

Heading back to the crew with an arm full of driftwood, the crew were piling the wood on the soft sand. One looked up, "We should have heaps of wood now."

Peter wrapped his arm around Blake drawing her closer as he kissed the side of her head. Ted's gaze connected with her eyes not saying anything as he turned back to the rest of the crew. "You had to do that in front of them all," she whispered, her cheeks blushing.

"What are you going to do about it?"

Reaching up to his ear, "I'll deal with you later."

"Noted," he replied tossing the wood near the fire pile.

As night fell, the bonfire lit up the beach. Dinner simmered away on the edge of the coals. Upbeat music added to the mood. The crew relaxed on the sand with their drinks in hand. With her nerves waning, Blake reclined against a log, the flames dancing in front of her. Her thoughts drifted back to the deployment when she looked back at fire with a different mindset. *If it wasn't for Tim giving me so much grief, I would have probably never met Peter*

Peter sat beside her, handing her a can of rum and cola. Taking a sip of her drink, Blake nestled against his chest as he draped his arm over her shoulder. "Cheers," he said, raising his beer to the crew.

"Cheers." A crew member looked back at Peter, "I always knew you two would hook up."

"Oh, you did not," Peter replied. Blake stared back at the flickering firelight with a smile and said nothing.

After dinner and a few drinks, the crew were drowsy. Blake and Peter paddled back to his boat. Trying to balance on a bouncing canoe while stepping onto a bobbing boat under the effect of a few drinks took coordination and a lot of laughter. Ducking to get through the small cabin doorway, Blake curled up next to Peter. Snuggled in his arms she stared across the bed not saying a thing.

"What are you thinking?" He asked, adjusting the covers.

"Bo going on holiday made me think of my promotion. How will we see each other if I'm sent to another city."

"Worry about that when it happens." He pulled her closer, "We came out here this weekend to have fun."

He is right. She rolled over, looking down at his alluring eyes, "Don't know about you, but I want some fun," she murmured. With her lips caressing his, her hair draped over his face as his hand searched for the light switch.

CHAPTER 11

HOLIDAYS AND HELL

Blake's brain hurt after spending the week cramming Bo's job requirements and procedures. *Which form goes in when?* She scribbled prompts across her notebook. *Let's see if I have this straight.* She ran her eyes down the page. *This is my last day to ask questions before he goes on holiday. Think woman.*

Friday, the day to send the weekly report to head office. Bo was out and about having given the job to Blake as practice. Working away, it was only now she noticed the wall fan randomly buzzed at annoying intervals. *Note, fix the fan.*

After a morning spent typing, she looked up from Bo's computer and called out, "Do you want to check the report before I send it."

Bo wandered back from the garage. Standing beside her, he ran his eyes down the screen. "You give more detail than I do."

Damn. "What should I change?"

"Nothing. Send it."

Done. Taking a deep breath, she pushed back in her chair, "What am I going to do if something goes wrong while you're away?"

"If? You mean when," he pulled the report out of the printer, "Ring Captain lover boy. He'll know what to do."

Lover boy? How professional is that? Hang on where is filing that report? Jotting down more notes, she asked, "Who is replacing me in the crew for the next two weeks?" She paused and looked back eyes wide. *No way!* Jumping to her feet she pointed her finger at Bo, "Don't say, Tim."

"You and Tim together. Ha. I wouldn't do that to the crew." He shuffled papers in the filing cabinet drawer, "He is long gone, they won't let him back here." Pushing the drawer closed, he leaned back against the desk, his tone and manner turned serious. "Control knows you're a member down, they will send in backup crews to incidents. How often do we attend incidents alone?"

"But—"

He leaned over the desk, patting her shoulder, "Look at this time as training for your promotion."

"If I get promoted," she groaned, arching her tight back muscles.

"It will happen, just don't stuff up for the next two weeks."

"No pressure," she pushed herself out of her chair and headed for the kitchen, "I need a coffee." *Just ring Lover Boy is his solution to a problem.* Glancing at her work phone. *I need to put Peter on speed dial.*

🚒 🚒

Two days into Bo's holidays, Blake sat in the fire truck passenger seat, heading toward a large column of black smoke rising in an older part of town. Running her eyes over the incident report. *A disused factory has caught fire. The police suspect squatters.* Numerous flashing lights randomly weaved in the traffic ahead. *Highgate crew has been assigned to a street at the far end of the building.* The ear-piercing squeal of sirens filled the air as they turned into the street.

"Crap, this place is huge." A derelict three-storey World War Two factory towered overhead and took up two city blocks. Finding a safe distance was difficult in the old narrow streets. The concrete and metal sheeting exterior walls were stained black with age. Smoke and flames were visible at the other end of the building in the next block.

Arriving at the scene, her heart was pounding. Sweat ran off her brow and she hadn't even got to the fire. This wasn't her first factory fire but it was her first big job as Captain. Scanning the meeting point her stomach was in knots. Some tension lifted off her shoulders seeing Peter and another Captain talking to a Commander on the same street. *I'm not alone, thank God.* Taking a deep breath, she reached for her helmet and whispered, "I can do this."

The fire started at the other end of the building and was spreading through the timber floors above. Peter took the lead and pulled up an old council plan of the building on his tablet screen. "We have to carry out a reconnaissance through these rooms looking for anyone who has not evacuated." Pointing to a line of rooms running off a main corridor.

Blake tightened her breathing mask and confirmed she had airflow. Scanning the crews, they all looked the same except for their helmets. *How am I meant to find my team in this lot?* The old external timber door had been kicked in too many times, a simple push had it swing open on a single hinge. Entering the building the air wasn't too smoky; it was thicker at the other end of the open space. A crashing thud came from behind. Blake jumped and spun around to see the last door hinge had let go.

The old broken glass windows overhead let in a limited amount of light for a short distance. Blake stopped inside the entrance and scanned the area; piles of old crates and unknown rubbish littered the open floor. In the distance, old graffiti-covered concrete columns held up the floor above. "Where is the corridor?" She asked over the radio.

"Must be an old plan," Peter replied. "Check those rooms in the far-left corner."

Blake entered one room with a crew member, and Peter checked the next. Flashing her torch around in the dark showed nothing but dust and cobwebs covering fifty-year-old junk. Whisps of smoke blended with the dust drifting in the air. Moving onto the biggest room in the centre of the space. It had stud walls on all sides, with a large blackboard on the far wall. Rows of old wooden desks and chairs lay scattered through the space like a classroom but with no sign of life.

"Check under the tables to be sure," Peter called out from inside the doorway. Blake was at the far end of the classroom looking under a desk when a series of distant booms made the ceiling shudder. A creaking groan overhead made her heart skip a beat as dust rained down in the torchlight.

"Evacuate!" Peter bellowed.

A cold terror ran over Blake's body as she instinctually yelled, "Evacuate," at the same time. Her pulse raced as she scrambled around the desks; the doorway still ten metres away. A cloud of dust rained down as the side wall peeled away, dropping the ceiling at a sharp angle. Ceiling tiles fell randomly, one bouncing off her helmet. *Crap.* "Get down!" She yelled diving under a desk.

The air was thick with dirt, fluff and other unknown stuff drifting to the floor. Darkness surrounded her, the only light came from her flashlight reflecting on nearby objects. Shining her flashlight around to see anything distant was marred by the raining dust. The groans and twang of steel snapping continued overhead. *We have to get out of here now.* Her pulse throbbed in her head as her breathing got heavier.

Time seemed to slow down as all her focus was on getting everyone to the exit. More ceiling panels fell behind her. "Peter!" she called out. The radio squealed back, her call not getting past the numerous other calls on the channel. She peered out from under the desk and saw someone under the next row of tables. Scurrying along on her hands and knees, she had to stop to free her air tank from an overhead desk drawer.

Meeting up with that crew member gave her a brief moment of relief. He came from the third team. *Where are the rest?* Her heart sank at seeing the pile of debris holding up the ceiling had also blocked the exit. Still looking for others they made their way toward the blocked exit. Garbled messages broke through on the radio. But she couldn't make it out.

Pulling aside the planks and ceiling bats from the exit, she heard yelling coming from the other side of the wall. *Keep digging.* Adrenaline had her body in full fight mode. She was joined by another crew member who found his way through the rumble. "How many crew were in here?" She asked.

"Three or Four, I don't know who escaped."

Where is my crew? A cold sweat broke out on her brow, not knowing who else was trapped in the room. Flashing the torch around the space she looked for any movement. The air was getting thicker with dust and smoke. *Where is the fire?* She started to throw items faster, causing some debris to topple over. "Take it easy," a crew member replied. Blake's air tank warning started beeping. *I'm almost out of air.* Conserving air was impossible with her rapid heart rate and scrambling to escape a collapsing building. Holding her breath, made her gasp more.

Her fear of being burnt alive was delayed as water started to rain down through the collapsed ceiling. *Great, make it collapse faster.* Grabbing her radio, she yelled, "Stop the—" A torch beam broke through the darkness from a hole in the debris. The bright light on her face made her wince and turn away. Someone outside had broken through under a roof beam. It didn't take long to clear an opening big enough for the crew to scramble out. Taking hold of the debris, she used all her strength to pull herself through the opening. A set of hands gripped her wrists firmly and pulled her free.

Her air tank alarm rang out constantly. Falling in a heap on the floor outside of the collapse, she ripped her mask off gasping for air. Dust still rained down around her making her cough. She didn't get time to recover when two crew grabbed her arms and dragged her toward the main exit door. Not having the energy to move, her boots carved tracks in the dust on the floor.

Peter stood in the external doorway counted heads and called out, "We have everyone." His eyes connected with hers, following her every move as she got hauled past him. It took a while for his words to register. *My crew was safe.*

Out on the street, Blake lay on the footpath staring up at the swirling black smoke in the sky. Still gasping for air, her whole body ached as the scale of the incident hit. Feeling light-headed she fought to stay conscious. A female paramedic dropped down beside her, wrapping an oxygen mask over her face. The woman's words were drowned out by all the sirens and yelling. Peter's head came into view above the paramedic. The sight of his face released a wave of emotion through her body. *He is not injured.* Tears welled in her eyes as she lost control of her feelings.

After a short while on oxygen, she felt slightly better. She pulled herself up, adjusting her oxygen mask, she stared back at the chaos around her. The crew's red, sweaty faces stood out against the cake of dust on their uniforms. As she looked back at the building, an outer wall slowly fell inward, followed by the roof seconds later. A cloud of dust, smoke and flames erupted from the area where they had just been rescued from. *Crap! We would be dead.* Her heart pounded as she gasped for air. Everything started to spin again as she laid back on the paving.

"Pull back," Peter bellowed over the noise. The able-bodied crews grabbed those still lying on the footpath and dragged them further up the street. Being held up by her arms, Blake's shins bounced over the kerbing. Nearby trucks rained water over the collapsing building as flames licked the sky.

Blake being one of numerous recovering crew members jammed on the narrow footpath, leaned against the bakery shop front. Emergency service personnel ran back and forth. The event was getting more chaotic by the second. *I should be helping them.* Taking deeper breaths of oxygen, Blake fought to regain her strength.

A paramedic jumped up and ran to a group after a crew member fell to the ground. Blake spun around pulling at her airline. One of the incident controllers approached and asked about what had happened inside the building. He ordered everyone in or near the collapse to be decontaminated as they didn't know what chemicals or substances were in the building.

Placing her full uniform in hazmat bags, the water pump started. *I only just got that uniform.* The reassurance that the person on the pump couldn't see anything, Blake still tried to hide her modesty while standing naked in the makeshift tent and being hosed down. Gasping as the cold water rained over her body only added to her shock of being overheated moments before. She shivered as goosebumps covered her body. *They could have found some warm water.*

Coming out of the shower someone handed her an old pair of fire overalls through the tent opening. The torn faded blue material had seen better days. The nametag caught her eye. *Doug.* Leaving the shower area, she was given a pair of cheap rubber slip-on shoes.

Those who had been decontaminated gathered in a nearby car-park. Blake sat huddled against a railing, still cold from the shower she could barely feel her heavy limbs. A support worker handed her two bottles of water, with the order to drink them both.

Peter crouched in front of her, rubbing her arms in an attempt to warm her up, "Are you Okay?"

Looking back in his eyes, he looked as bad as she felt. She nodded, "I'll survive."

"Let's make sure." A bus pulled up beside them. Peter turned to the group, "We have orders to go to the hospital for a check-up." Turning back to Blake he grabbed her hands pulling her to her feet.

🚌 🚌

Everyone sat quietly in the hospital waiting room. One of many in a queue waiting to be called into the doctor's room, Blake sat wrapped in a blanket, sipped her coffee and stared blankly at the floor. Peter sat down beside her, "Feeling better?"

"I don't know yet," she mumbled.

"Not bad for your second day as Captain," he forced a smile, trying to lift her mood.

"I don't know if I'm cut out for Captain," she groaned.

He slid his arm behind her back, drawing her nearer. "Hey, we were all thrown in the deep end with this job." He leaned towards her ear and whispered, "I thought I lost you."

Those haunting words reinforced her thoughts about how close they came to dying. "Don't say that," she mumbled as tears ran down her face.

"I'm sorry," He murmured, wrapping his arms around her. She buried her face in his chest and sobbed not caring who saw their embrace.

A few hours later, after a lot of talking and further checks, all three teams were stood down for the next twenty-four hours. Most of the equipment and vehicles had been returned to their stations and packed away by the able-bodied crew. Blake spent most of the trip back to work on the phone with the head office going over everything.

CHAPTER 12

NEXT MOVE

Leaving work, Blake hurried home, taking no time to jump in the shower. The hot steaming water reversed the muscle stiffness caused by the cold fire hose. She leaned against the wall, letting the soothing water run over her body. Images of the collapse ran through her mind as she tried to work out what she had done wrong. Her phone continuously rang on the vanity outside. Grabbing a towel, she roughly patted herself dry. *Peter wants to be let in.* Wrapped in the towel, dripping water across her floor she pushed the button to let him into her floor.

There were a couple of knocks on the door moments later. *He is here.* Opening the door, he stepped inside, stopping as she threw her arms around him. Their bodies together in a firm embrace, tears welled in her eyes. Easing back, he brushed her wet hair behind her ear, "Are you all right?"

"Not really. What about you?"

"I'm Okay."

Peter closed the door behind him. Cradling her face in his hands he looked deep into her eyes as tears welled in his.

"Stop that," she ordered. *I can't handle him breaking down now.*

He leaned in with a warm kiss and a big hug. After a minute, her cheek being squashed against his chest made it hard to breathe, she mumbled, "Can I dry off."

Blake left the bathroom in a robe to meet Peter in the hall. Reaching in for another hug, "I we were dead—" her hands started shaking.

Peter pulled her in tighter, "You're alive. We are safe. Stop thinking about it."

Wiping her cheek, "But—"

"Don't make me have to deal with you again," he looked back with a cheeky grin.

She pulled back and forced a smile, "Want to go fishing tomorrow?"

"No, they want us to stay home in case of delayed shock or if they have questions."

"Shouldn't you be home then?"

"No, I'm not leaving you alone tonight," he looked down at his old overalls covered in water from her embrace. "Can I have a shower and get out of these clothes?"

She looked back at the name tag on his faded emergency clothes, "Sure. Buzz?"

"Don't ask me where they got this stuff from."

He wandered out of the bathroom with the towel wrapped around his hips. His toned abs and chest hair still looked good. "I don't have any clothes to wear," he said.

"Why didn't you get some from home before you came here."

"I came straight from work."

"Well, my shirts won't fit you, do you want me to drop past your place and get some?"

"No, you need rest. I'll drop over there later." He leaned back on the couch in his towel, "I should bring spare clothes over for next time."

Blake reached over the back of the couch, leaning with a kiss she handed him her phone, "Here order something for dinner. I'll get us drinks," she headed to the kitchen. Returning with a soda in each hand she sat beside him, she leaned against his shoulder, "It took long enough to get my new pants from stores last time. I'm back to having three pairs of work pants."

"Least of our worries," he replied placing her phone on the side table.

"What do you mean?" She looked back confused.

"You'll have to deal with the delivery guy. I have no clothes."

🚌 🚌

The dust kept falling, and the air alarm rang out in her ears drowning out the panic in her head. Blake's jumped; eyes wide she glanced at the clock. *3 AM.* Unable to sleep, she tossed and turned. Peter rolled over wrapping his arms around her. Safe in his embrace she took hold of his hand, her fingers entwined with his. "Every time I close my eyes, I'm back in the rubble, fighting to escape with no air." She started breathing heavily, a lump grew in her throat as the fear rushed over her body.

Peter held her tighter with one arm and flicked through his phone bringing up some relaxing music with the other. He rested his hand on her jaw, turning her face to his, "Look at me." His gaze was strong. "I catch more fish than you do. What are you going do about that?"

What the hell? Her mind went blank for a moment, "You suck a counselling," she groaned.

"I don't have any caramels on me. I'm all you have," he drew her closer, kissing the top of her head as she tucked her head against his chest.

The sound of his pounding heart gave her some comfort. "Before Bo went on holiday he said if I had any problems to ring you. I'm guessing that didn't include counselling."

"Sorry." He shuffled to a better position and started talking about the enjoyable memories of his life as a firefighter. When he got to recent history, he described meeting her on deployment after her problems with Tim.

Her memories of the deployment filled her mind, the nights sitting in the dark talking with a stranger she had met in the smoke. A warm feeling rose inside her as she snuggled closer. His reassuring embrace, slowed her pulse as she calmed down. With her adrenaline spent, her eyes grew heavy.

The sun peeking through the blinds arrived too soon. Blake yawned, rolled over and went to sit up. Peter wrapped his arm around her drawing her against his body. "Where are you going? We have the day off."

"Toilet."

Leaving the bathroom, Blake staggered down the hall to Peter up about and making coffee. "You look like you need more sleep," she said leaning on the counter.

"Have you looked in the mirror?"

"Yep, unfortunately."

He chuckled and leaned in for a kiss, "Still look good."

"Shut up and give me coffee," she groaned.

"Kiss first."

Sitting at the table, Blake stared blankly at the table, sipping her coffee. After a few mouthfuls, she asked, "What are you doing today?"

"Not much, go home and get some clothes. You probably should go back to bed."

Back at work two days later, the rest of the week was spent on the phone talking to head office, HR, counsellors and Peter regularly checking up on her. After reliving the week and the collapse in the head office report, she looked forward to fishing over the weekend.

🚌 🚌

Saturday evening. Blake sat alone on the back of the boat, bobbing up and down in the moonlight. The fishing rod hung low in her hands. She suspected the large tug on the line earlier took her bait but getting new bait required moving. Gazing out at the rising full moon, the seas sparkled. A relaxing ballad drifted on the breeze behind her. The dim flashlight in the cabin made the darkness relaxing.

Peter sat down beside her, "Have some dessert," handing her a wrapped ice cream cone with one hand and taking her fishing rod with the other. Winding in the reel ended with a cut line. "That one got away," he said placing the rod to the side. Sliding his arm behind her back, he asked, "What are you thinking about?"

"Not much."

"That's a lot of thinking for not much," he leaned in closer, "Are you still going over the collapse?"

She dipped her head, "I didn't know where anyone was. You, the crew, anyone."

His gentle touch rubbing her back eased some of her tension, "We are all safe."

"I would never forgive myself if I lost any of you." A knot grew in her chest and tears welled in her eyes.

Peter got to his feet and headed back to the boat cabin. She glanced over her shoulder, "Are you Okay?"

He returned, easing down beside her and handed her a plain envelope.

"What's this?"

"Open it. Oh, move away from the water first."

Turning to the centre of the boat she pulled out a set of keys and a piece of paper with numbers written on it. She blankly looked back through the dim light. "Keys?"

"We spend most of our nights together. Save your money and move in with me."

Move in with him. Her heart rate increased, and she lunged forward wrapping her arms around him.

"I wouldn't have left you in the collapse," he whispered.

All her pent-up feelings for the week rose to the surface as tears ran down her cheeks. Her embrace got stronger as she pulled his body against hers. Sobbing she buried her face into his shoulder. Sitting together alone at sea, their embrace went on. The sea breeze blew her hair in his face, causing him to brush her hair to the side. Over time she calmed down and pulled back. Peter, tidied her hair, gazing back at her. "So, when do you want to move in?"

She sat back, wiping her face, "My rent is paid till the end of the month." The notepaper flipped up into the wind circling overhead and blew out to sea. "Crap," she swung her hand out to catch it but missed.

"Don't worry about that."

"What were the numbers?"

"The PIN to my security system," he rose to his feet, "I can write them out again."

"What now?"

"No, I'm going to bed. Are you coming?"

"In a minute," she looked back as he disappeared below deck. Sitting in the silence with the evening breeze blowing past her face, a stillness ran over her body. The keys rattled as they landed on the deck beside her. *Don't lose them overboard.* She scooped up the keys, shuffling them in her hands. *Move in with him?* Her memories recalled their time together. *Yes, he's a keeper.* A warmth grew inside as she straightened her shoulders, rose and headed below deck.

🚌 🚌

The second week was quiet, Blake sent the weekly report, collapsing back in her chair and taking a deep breath. *Bo is back next week.* She pulled the page out of the printer. *It's a shorter report than last week's report.* Most of the content last week was based around the factory fire. This week was pretty quiet carrying out maintenance. *I think fire control has us at the bottom of the call-out list after the collapse.*

While busy being a Captain, her thoughts drifted to what she needed to do to move house. Thinking back to his home and where she would fit in her stuff. *His lounge is better than my old thing. Sell it. His house has three bedrooms, which is enough for my one-bed apartment to fit into.*

Friday afternoon, Captain duties were over. Blake sat at her dining table sipping her beer, and her eyes slowly ran around the room.

What am I going to do with all this? How am I going to move it? Her gaze stopped at the TV. *I'll give that to work to replace that old black and white TV in the lunch room. And what am I going to do with that?* She scribbled some notes on her notebook and crossed one out again. *Stuff this.* She grabbed her phone and invited Peter over to dinner and a planning session on moving house.

CHAPTER 13

STEP UP

Blake kicked back in the passenger seat, glad to be back as a crew member now that Bo had returned from holidays. The crew arrived back at the fire station after spending the morning checking fire hydrants. It's a simple job but climbing in and out of the truck continuously made her legs ache. Standing on the bottom step she reached over to grab her kit off the seat. Stepping down onto the floor, she paused. *Oh, no.* Out of the corner of her eye, Bo walked out of the office towards her with a director from the head office beside him. *What has Tim said now? No, I stuffed up as Captain?* She grabbed her kit and headed for the locker room.

"Blake, have you got a moment?" Bo asked.

"Can it wait till I have a shower?"

"No."

Great. She turned meeting them both near the truck. Slumping her shoulders, "What have I done now?"

The director stepped forward, "Nothing. Bo has been promoted to the district office," he paused, "And I'm here to see if you want his old posting."

Her heart skipped a beat. Taken off guard her kit bag fell to the floor, she froze, and her eyes widened. *What? I didn't stuff up as Captain.* She took a step, "Captain. At this station?"

"Yes."

Her heart pounded in her chest, she put all her focus on controlling her emotions. *My promotion.* "Yes." *And I don't have to move towns.*

"Great. The posting will take effect in a month. Captain Bosham will spend this time training you for the job."

"Okay, thank you." Her nerves tingled as the director held out his hand.

"Congratulations Captain Davis."

Captain Davis! Her inner voice screamed.

After a quick nod, the director turned back to Bo, "I'm late for a meeting. We will talk next week."

Blake and Bo stood in the garage entrance watching the director's car merge with the traffic. Blake glanced across at Bo, "Yes," pumping her fist. Regaining some composure, "Oh, congratulations on your promotion too."

"Go for a shower, Captain Davis," he replied with a smile.

Dashing into the bathroom, she had to let her excitement out. Dialling Peter, her feet tapped a little dance waiting for him to answer.

"Hi, what's happened?"

Taking a deep breath, "Bo has been promoted to district."

"So—"

"I'm replacing him as Captain." Her words got quicker as she went along.

"You've been promoted?"

"Yes," her voice went hoarse as she tried to hold back her excitement in the bathroom.

"Cool, drinks after work it is."

Refreshed from the shower, she skipped out of the bathroom, her smile beaming. A crew member came out of the kitchen, "Had a good night last night?"

She paused with her hands on her hips, trying to show some authority, she replied, "Is that how you talk to your new Captain?"

"About bloody time," he replied with a friendly hug.

Blake took hold of Peter's hand as they entered the pub laughing and still full of elation from the day's achievement. Approaching the bar, the overhead lights reflected off a familiar face. *Alex?* She leaned towards Peter, "Did you invite your crew?"

"And yours."

"Why?"

"Hello, this is the best thing that has happened to us all in a while. Time to celebrate," he headed for the crew leaning on the bar, "There is a reason I got a taxi tonight? We are partying."

"I was going to suggest we move my furniture tomorrow," she replied.

"We are all here, we will work it out," he turned to the bartender, "A bottle of champagne and two glasses."

The month of training went fast. Blake stepped out of her car, gazing back at the station. Her chest was tight with mixed feelings of pride and anxiety around her first day as the new Captain of Highgate Station. John's crew were still finishing up from the night shift. Blake arrived earlier than usual to settle in before being thrown into a fire call. With coffee in hand, she eased back into her chair. She rearranged the desk while waiting for the computer to boot up. Removing Bo's old name plaque from the front of the desk, she filed it in the bottom drawer. The crew wandered in and stood at the door staring back at her without saying anything. "What's up?" She asked, looking back confused,

They shrugged their shoulders. "Just checking out at our new boss," Troy replied casually.

"Yeah, what do you want us to do?" Asked another.

Leaning forward, she replied, "The same thing you do every morning. Or do you want me to say drop and give me fifty push-ups?"

"No, we're good." They shuffled, nodded and went about their business.

Blake turned back to her computer screen. Some idle chatter filtered through the doorway. "Fifty Push-ups? Show them who is the boss," Bo's chuckle rang out. Startled she glanced up, Bo and a director stood inside the doorway.

"Bo. What's happening?" She asked jumping to her feet.

"Just driving by."

So, you were just driving by. "And?"

The director stepped forward handing her a piece of paper, "Dean at the academy has a couple of graduates that would suit your replacement in the crew."

Running her eyes down the page showed a brief resume of three rookie firefighters. *I get replaced with a rookie?* "Couldn't you just have emailed me?"

Bo leaned back against the door, "We were just driv—"

"Driving by, yeah, yeah."

"Do you have any questions or problems?" The director asked.

"I have just started."

The director turned to Bo, "I think we will leave her to settle in."

With the bosses gone, Blake eased back into her chair reaching for her coffee and opened her email program. Running her eyes over the long list of emails scrolling down the screen. *Damn hasn't Bo, check his mail in weeks. So much junk.* One email caught her eye as the phone rang. *Hell, who now.* She shoved her phone under her ear as she read a safety notification. "Yes."

"Yes?" Peter replied hesitantly. "Good morning, Captain Davis. Has your first day started that well?"

Sighing, "Sorry. It's been busy and it hasn't even started."

"Welcome to being a Captain," he laughed.

"Did you ring for a reason?"

"Not really. It can wait," he muttered.

"Can we talk later—" the fire siren rang out through the station, "Damn!" She threw herself back in her seat, tossing her pen across the desk.

"Chill, I just got the same alarm. See you on the battleground."

🚒 🚒

With dinner over, Blake walked out of the bathroom, pulled her bathrobe tight and dropped down on the couch, silently flicking through the TV channels. Peter handed her a wine as he sat beside her. "Was the day that bad? You're not saying much."

She turned toward him, "At the fire today, what did Alex mean when he said *with you out of town?*"

He shuffled, "I rang to tell you this morning, but it wasn't a good time for you. I have been asked to help train the new captain at Dickson." He moved closer, "You know the station where the captain had a heart attack."

Not believing what she had just heard, her eyes widened and she replied in a raised voice, "You're moving to Dickson?"

"No. No, it's temporary," he shuffled in his seat, placing his beer on the side table.

"How long for?"

"Two weeks, I'll be home on the weekend," he placed his hand on hers, "You get the house to yourself for two weeks."

Don't try to put a positive twist on not being here. "You want me to water the garden," she mumbled.

"Go out with girls. Whatever, as long as you are happy." He straightened his back, "I will call you every night."

Blake looked away as she rose and headed toward the kitchen, not saying anything.

Peter turned on some relaxing music and came up behind her, "Talk to me."

"It's been a hectic day," she turned and leaned back on the bench "When are you leaving?"

Looking back at her gaze, he slipped his hands around her waist, "Sunday night, back Friday night."

Glancing to the side, "Who will I call if I have a problem?"

"Me, John, hell Bo would still help you." The soft touch of his fingers gripped her chin turning her face back to his. "It will be all right," his eyes connected with hers as he leaned in with a kiss to her forehead, "Grab your drink. Let's watch a movie."

🚒 🚒

I'm getting hungry, must be lunchtime. Blake glanced at her watch. *Two hours, they should be back by now.* She wandered into the radio room, calling the truck and getting no reply. *What are they doing?* Pulling out her phone. *Troy, let's see if he has his phone on him.* Leaning in the doorway, with her phone to her ear she listened to the dial tone repeating until it timed out. She returned to the radio room, calling the truck one more time.

"We are almost back," Troy replied.

"You're late."

The sound of the truck motor filled the garage. Blake left the room stopping dead at the back of the garage. *What the?* The back corner of the truck was caved in making the overhead ladder sit at an angle. Moving around the driver's side the back hatch was held closed with several pieces of black duct tape. The driver's door opened, and Blake looked up wide-eyed, "What the hell happened."

"A van ran a red light."

"Is everyone Okay?"

"Yeah, we barely felt it."

Blake returned to the back of the truck, gazing at the white paint smear over the red panel, "And the white van?"

"Total write-off," Troy came alongside, "The police got all the details."

Hell. Blake wiped the sweat from her brow, "I have to ring Bo." Heading back to the office she turned back to Troy, "You said they ran a red light?"

"Yeah, they couldn't see a big red fire engine. What hope did they have of seeing a light red light," he chuckled.

Oh, very funny. Raising her eyebrows she turned back to the office not saying anything.

Hanging up, she stared back at the phone. *Bo seemed pretty casual about the whole problem. Now where do I find a form fifty-two?* The computer beeped as a new email appeared on the screen. *Form Fifty-two.* Waiting for the form to come out of the printer, she read the last line of the email saying, "Take the truck to Stevens, he is expecting you now."

Just how fast does Bo operate? How many trucks get involved in accidents regularly?

🚒 🚒

Blake chopped the onions for her steak when the phone rang. *He's early tonight.* The conversation started as usual until she explained the day's activities.

"Form fifty-two," Peter replied

"Had your share of accidents," she asked.

"It's normal," his voice softened, "How did you handle it?"

"I rang Bo. And had a vodka after work."

"Oh, it's not your fault. Chill, destress, go shopping. Whatever you girls do to feel better," Peter said.

Blake chuckled, "You have no idea what we do."

"Nope. I don't think I want to know."

Tucking her phone under her ear, she scooped the onions into the pan beside her overcooked steak. "I'm burning dinner, I'll call you later."

"It's Okay, I have smoke alarms," he laughed, pausing as he came back in a quieter voice, "Don't burn down my house."

☗ ☗

Friday evening, Blake settled down to dinner when the phone rang. *Peter.* "Hey darl, I'm an hour away. How was your day?"

"Pretty quiet, I got some shopping done at lunch," she glanced at the lingerie store packaging near the bin.

"Cool, see you soon."

The hour ticked over; Blake sat at the table reading the latest magazine. Her attention was drawn to the driveway as Peter's vehicle parked out front. A growing excitement inside her made her smile. The door sprung open as he greeted her with open arms and a bunch of multicoloured flowers.

Her eyes widened at the flowers as their bodies embraced. Following a tender kiss, he stepped back presenting the flowers with a big smile. His eyes darted from her face down to her robe as he ran his hand over the silken material, "Is that new? I haven't seen that before"

"Yes," she smiled returning to the kitchen to get a vase, "Have you had dinner?"

"I had it at the roadhouse. I need a shower." Peter replied as he ran back down the stairs to get his bags.

Refreshed after his trip, Peter pulled his towel tight around his hips as he approached her in the hall. She dropped the robe off her shoulder, flicking her hair aside to reveal a lace strap on her bare shoulder. Looking deeply into his eyes she murmured, "You said you liked red."

Peter stopped mid-step; his eyes wide as his attention was totally on her. Wrapping his arms around her, he drew her nearer. Slowly running his fingers over her shoulder, "I will have to investigate this further," he replied in a deep smooth voice.

CHAPTER 14

MEMORABLE CRUISE

Captain Blake tidied her office at the end of another week. *Crap.* Her eyes followed her cup of pens hitting the floor, scattering pens under her desk. On her hands and knees, she strained to reach a pen in the groove in the back corner of her desk. A reverberating buzz echoed around her setting her teeth on edge. *My phone.* Jumping, she shuffled backwards, whacking her head on the drawer. A stinging pain radiated across her skull. *Crap, that hurt.*

Rubbing the back of her head, she put on a forced happiness waiting for the pain to subside, "Hi, Pete,"

"Captain Davis," his deep voice resonated down the phone, smoother than usual.

Oh, that's formal. "Yes, Captain Sycamore," she eased back into her seat.

"Congratulations, six months at the top."

"Six months. That went fast," she glanced at her desk calendar. *Six months and I'm still alive.*

"I have booked dinner for seven to celebrate. Wear something fancy."

"Fancy?" The excitement had her shuffle in the chair. "Seven, I better get home and prepare."

Hanging up the phone, she bent over picking up the pen cup, her eyes drifting toward the underside of the desk. *Stuff it, it will still be there next week.*

🚌 🚌

Checking her earrings, she glanced at her watch. *Where is he? He said he booked dinner for seven. It's a quarter to seven and he isn't home yet. Should I ring him?* A car roared up the driveway. *He is here.* Looking in the mirror, Blake fluffed her hair and smoothed her lipstick.

Peter ran past her, "Hi, dear." Not stopping as he dived into the shower. Returning a short while later, pulling his evening jacket over his unbuttoned shirt. His bare chest and abs stood out over his slacks.

"That looks fancy," she replied buttoning up his shirt as he slicked back his wet hair. Leaning in for a quick kiss, she straightened his collar.

Slipping on his shoes, he looked up from the lounge. His eyes ran over her black evening dress, stockings and heels. "Wow, you look good."

Glad you finally noticed. Grabbing her purse, they headed out the door at seven. Peter slipped around the passenger door opening it as she approached. *He is putting it on tonight. What is he up to?*

"Where are we going?"

"That's a surprise."

Her insides were twisted in knots. *Is he planning? No, don't go there.* She glanced back with a nervous grin as he headed into town.

110

Peter rested his hand on her thigh, "Chill, it's just dinner."

The carpark was full of luxury cars, and Peter's Ranger felt out of place as she stepped out onto the pavement. With Peter on her arm, she entered the dining room. Numerous wall lights and table candles added atmosphere to the darkness. Blake took a seat at a table for two, the waiter filled their glasses with champagne. She ran her eye over the menu. *Lobster in white wine sauce and capers.* Her eyes widened. *Is that the price? It's one of those restaurants. I had to dress fancy to get in the door. But why does he want to come here?*

"See anything you like?" He asked running an eye over the menu.

"I'll have the duck in red wine tortellini and cheese sauce." *That shouldn't bankrupt us.*

The meal had been ordered; the candlelight flickered on his face. He had a nervous energy, and he wasn't saying much. *Stuff this.* She reached across the table, "What is all this about? Talk to me."

He reached into his jacket pocket and pulled out a ten-inch parcel, passing it across the table, "Congratulations, Captain Davis."

The present was wrapped simply in plain blue paper held together with tape. Her eyes rose to connect with his gaze. *Not what I was expecting.*

"Open it."

Peeling open one end, she pulled out a white sundress with a blue tropical flower print and a separate ticket. *All-day cruise and fishing charter.* Taking hold of his hand, "Thank you. A fishing charter."

"We have to be there by nine tomorrow morning."

"Tomorrow," she glanced at the ticket and back to the dress. "Am I meant to be fishing in this?" The soft fabric of the sundress draped from her fingers.

"Yes, it's a cruise with staff. I don't want other blokes stealing you in a bikini," he grinned raising his glass.

She chuckled sipping her champagne. *I could have worn my fishing gear. There's nothing sexy about that.*

🚌 🚌

Climbing out of Peter's car, Blake straightened her dress. *Sundress and sandals. I have never worn this fishing ever.* She stepped onto the timber marina, a large cruise boat sat at the end of the jetty. Its double-height cabin towered over the smaller boats nearby. *That is pretty big for the two of us.*

Peter stepped alongside draping his arm over her shoulder "What do you think?"

"It's overkill for some fishing."

He glanced back with a beaming smile, "Come on, we are late."

Climbing on board they were greeted by a cruise attendant. A small crowd were out on the sun deck chatting. *Makes sense, we are not alone on a cruise.* Wandering into the dining area, fruit platters and nibblies lined the far wall. She looked at the bottles of liquor on the bar's back wall, leaning towards Peter, "This is more of a Christmas Party than a fishing trip."

"So, let's celebrate. What are you drinking?" He asked.

Alcohol before lunch? "Water will do."

"We are here to have fun, champagne please," he said to the bartender.

Blake collected her glass of champagne. A woman stepped up beside her at the bar followed by a male. Blake glanced back before taking a second look. "Ted?" She looked back at Peter, confused.

Peter, turned facing them both reaching and shaking the woman's hand, "Kystal, Ted, glad you could make it." Peter leaned towards Blake, "Our crews and their partners were invited too."

What the? Blake looked back at his calm face, and her eyes widened. Her pulse increased as she scanned the crowd. *Mark, Troy, Liam, crap, they are all here.* "What's the occasion?"

"Can't we all celebrate your six-month milestone as Captain," sliding his arm behind her back, "Come on, let's meet everyone."

Moving out into the sun, the sea breeze picked up as the boat pulled out of the harbour. Scanning the group, some of the faces were familiar. *So many names to remember.* Her eyes paused at one woman. *He didn't.* Blake leaned into Peter's ear and whispered, "You invited Gail?"

"No, Alex invited her. He likes her CPR apparently," Peter whispered back.

After about an hour of chatting the attendants brought out platters of food and bottles of champagne before one attendant approached Peter, "We are ready for you."

Lunch. Great I'm starving. Blake looked back from the side rail as Peter stepped forward.

"Can I have everyone inside?"

Attendants handed out glasses of champagne as they entered the cabin making Blake's nerves tingle. *What is going on? Is he? No, I thought that at the dinner last night and it didn't happen.*

Everyone in the room had a glass except for Peter. He stood beside Blake silent as his eyes roamed her face. Sweat started to form on his brow as he took hold of her hand.

He looks nervous. She looked up at his face before glancing sideways at the group. They were all looking back at them both. *What the hell?* Her pulse increased and her eyes followed his deep gaze as he dropped to a knee. *Crap!* A stabbing pain hit her chest. Her eyes widened as she held her breath.

"Blake Davis, will you do me the honour of becoming my wife?" In his hand, a medium size diamond with a gold band.

Her gaze flashed to the ring and back at his warm smile. Tears of joy filled her eyes, "Yes."

Taking hold of her hand, he slipped the ring on her finger before wrapping his arms around her in a firm embrace. With her head buried in his chest the cheers of the guest were partly muffled.

"Where's the kiss," Ted called out.

His warm lips meeting hers added to her rising fire inside. Taking a deep breath, she wrapped her arms around him again, firmly holding his body against hers.

"Look at me," one of the wives called out with a camera in hand.

Blake wiped her eyes while trying to hide her flushed cheeks. They turned facing the numerous cameras clicking away.

"Thank you, everyone, lunch is served," Peter said as he turned back to Blake for another warm hug and kiss.

Receiving hugs from everyone, Blake's stomach grumbled. Reaching the last person, she was eager to get some lunch as the alcohol on her empty stomach was making her light-headed. Joining the others at the buffet, she filled her plate. Looking around to find Peter, he was in the corner still getting congratulations from his crew.

Sitting on the side deck, Blake peeled her prawns and turned to Peter, "What happened to our fishing?"

"We haven't got there yet. Priorities, would you rather I proposed when you were tired and covered in fish."

Leaning her head on his shoulder, "No. This is perfect, thank you."

🚎 🚎

Pulling up near a large reef, the water was alive with movement. A rising excitement ran over the group, some were more excited than others as they had never seen reef fish before. Peter walked over to Blake handing her a bag.

Taking it from his hand, Blake asked, "What's this?"

"Your fishing gear. You can't wear that fishing."

Cheeky bugger.

He held out his hand, "Give me the ring, we don't want it getting covered in fish on the first day." With the ring safely back in its case he slipped it back in his bag.

One group joined Blake and Peter fishing over the side of the boat, while others snorkelled with a diver at the back. There was a small group not interested in either activity, they spent the day relaxing.

The afternoon had been packed with action. Blake leaned on the foredeck handrail as the cruise headed for port. Silently staring out at the horizon, her hair dancing in the sea breeze. An arm wrapped around her back as Peter leaned against her shoulder. "How are you going?"

"Just chilling," she glided her arm behind his back, "It's been a big day." She pulled out her phone taking a picture of them both.

Showing the photo to Peter, he turned to face her, "Now, that's why I bought the dress. Did you want that outfit in your engagement photo?"

Not my green cargo gear. "No, dear. Good planning."

Seeing the marina come into view was a relief. One last group hug as everyone dragged their tired bodies ashore. Blake slumped back in the passenger seat, looking across to Peter's warm smile, she reached out, "I enjoyed today. Do you have fun?"

"Yes," taking hold of her hand, "Let's get home and get cleaned up."

She waved her fingers in front of him, "Where's my ring?"

He retrieved the case from behind the seat, took hold of her hand and slid the ring on her finger. Her face lit up; she leaned in for a slow kiss.

Back home, showered and relaxing over dinner, Peter asked, "Have looked inside the band?"

Inside? "No," she slipped the ring off her finger. A series of engraved numbers ran around inside the band. *It's not the date.* She studied it closer, "What does it mean?"

"Recognise the first five numbers?"

She held it up to the light and looked closer, "My work ID number?"

"Yes. And the next five are mine. Joined as one."

"We aren't joined as one yet." *He looks very pleased with himself.* Slipping the ring back on her finger, "You were confident I was going to say yes. It would be hard to use this ring for someone else."

"I knew what you would say."

116

"Guess what I'm going to say now," She rose, getting a drink of water from the kitchen, "I'm going to bed. And I'm sleeping in tomorrow."

He rose to his feet and wrapped his hands around her waist as she passed, "Not without a goodnight kiss."

CHAPTER 15

CHANGE OF PLANS

Blake handed Peter a piece of pizza as she reclined on the couch. All his attention focused on the unfolding news on the TV. *The wild-fires have started early this year. Oh great, that forest took over a month to control the last time it went up.* Images of luxury timber houses amongst the forest trees flashed on the screen. *Why do people build so close to stuff that will burn down their prize posses-sions?* "Here we go again. And I just bought a new pot plant, too," Blake muttered, reaching for her glass of wine.

Keeping his eyes fixed on the screen Peter replied, "I bought a self-watering pot for it." He reached out sliding his arm over her shoulder, "See, I will make a good father."

Really. She glanced out of the corner of her eye, "Leaving the kids home with plenty of food and water is hardly good parenting."

"Eat your pizza," he replied, returning to the news.

🚒 🚒

Making her way through the early morning traffic, Blake's phone buzzed before she had even arrived at work. *Prepare for a deployment on Saturday the sixteenth. What! That's the date of my wedding!* A lump developed in her throat and she pulled into the station carpark.

Scrambling out of the car with her kit bag under one arm, she had her phone to her ear, "Peter, have you been notified of a deployment?"

"Yeah. Good timing."

Roughly scribbling her signature on the time log, "But our wedding," she replied. Scurrying into the office she changed her phone to the other ear as she dropped her bag on the chair. Leaning over the desk, she flicked on her computer and headed toward the kitchen.

"We can postpone it to a day after we get back," he replied with some background thuds.

"The season has only just started. We could be postponing this thing continuously for months," she replied shoving her cup under the coffee machine.

"I'll call the celebrant and change it to this weekend."

"This weekend! I'll have to call everyone."

"Who? There's your crew, my crew and my mother," he said, "I can pull her out of the home anytime."

And Trish. Her tight shoulders eased. *Our wedding is not that complicated. With no relatives left alive, and a quiet wedding in the park there is nothing to panic about.* "You're right, let's do it."

Returning to her office with her coffee, Blake dropped into her seat and scribbled a to-do list for the week ahead. Looking back at the long list she realised her workload had doubled, bringing her wedding forward and preparing for deployment at the same time. *Oh, bugger.* Running down the list, she placed a cross next to some tasks. *The crew can do them.*

A short time later, she hung up the phone and crossed another task off the list. Partway through dialling the next number, the fire sirens rang out through the station. *Oh, I don't have time for fires.* She grabbed her gear and hurried out the door. Pulling the truck door closed, the sirens wailed to create a break in the traffic. *Group meeting on the way.* "Everyone, we are being deployed on the sixteenth so the wedding is this weekend. Fifteen hundred hours in the park. The hall was booked out, so we'll have drinks at our place afterwards."

"Cool. What about the fire we are heading towards?" Troy asked.

"Oh, yeah. A vent over a flare grill has set alight to a cafe roof."

🚒 🚒

Peter spent the night at Ted's. He claims it's the whole seeing the bride before the wedding tradition. I think it has more to do with having some pleasant surprises on the day. Blake kept her nerves at bay by packing her bag for deployment. *What a honeymoon, back to the fires. I'm going to want a good trip away afterwards for my honeymoon.* Her alarm rang out. *Time to get ready, don't want to be too late for my wedding.*

Blake straightened her off-white evening gown as she got out of the car. Hoping on one leg, she struggled to get her heels on in the carpark. Trish and two of the crew wives joined her as bridesmaids. One maid handed her a bunch of white roses after fixing the gold ribbon binding them, while another tidied her hair. Slowly walking down the path, classical music played on a nearby speaker. A small group of unknown civilians gathered under a nearby tree to watch. *Who doesn't love a wedding?* Peter and both crews were in their navy blue formal fire uniforms. *A very fancy touch to a casual wedding in the park.* As the crews turned toward her their epaulettes and silver buttons glistened in the sunlight. A line of official-looking firefighters stood out against the garden backdrop. *Bright, I should have worn more jewellery.* As she got closer, Peter turned toward her, his smile beaming and his eyes sparkled.

After a short ceremony, everyone moved into the rose garden for photos. A group photo with Peter's mother happened early so her caregiver could take her home.

With everyone loaded up in the cars, they headed off for Peter's place. Reaching the main road, they all turned left, "Where are we going? Our house is that way." Blake asked, looking over her shoulder.

"One more photo," Peter replied.

A short distance later they all pulled up in front of Highgate station. They all gathered on the driveway in front of the fire trucks. Peter and his crew stretched out on the right with Blake and her crew on the left. A long line of rank and ceremony framed against the grand old station and two majestic engines. These photos had more of an air of formality than the rose garden pictures. A uniting of two fire stations. The bridesmaids stayed out of the all-fire brigade photos. *Being the only female out of uniform with an army of firefighters in uniform feels like I'm marrying the mob.* A line of firefighters and a bride standing out front of a fire station drew the attention of the general public. Blake tried to keep a sweet smile posing for photos with cheers and whistles from passers-by. "Get this over with," she whispered.

"Just one more," the photographer replied waving to one of her crew who returned moments later with Blake's formal Captain's jacket and hat. Peter draped the jacket over her shoulders and carefully slipped her dress hat over her hair. Everyone lined up for another group shot before the bridal couple stood in front of a truck alone. With the photo session over, Blake returned to her office, and slid the jacket off her shoulders, "Not exactly regulation," she replied easing her hat off her head.

"You're not running for president. I ran it past the director. He approved the whole thing." Peter brushed aside a few of her stray hairs from removing her hat. "The head office wants a picture for the newspaper."

"Newspaper?" Placing her jacket on the hanger, "So much for a simple private wedding."

He took hold of her hands, "Who doesn't love a feel-good story," he glanced over his shoulder to the crew hanging around. "Let's go back to our place and party."

As she reached for her office door handle, he took hold of her waist drawing her nearer, "Smile, Mrs Sycamore."

She smiled and leaned in for a loving kiss. Pulling the door closed, the name on the door caught her eye. *Captain Davis. I will have to change that. This is not where I expected to be twelve months ago.*

Peter looked back, "What's the problem?"

"The door says Captain Davis. I have to change it."

"You don't have to change it. It is up to you."

He is leaving it up to me to decide if I keep my surname or take on his. I should send Tim a thank you card. Lifting the hem of her dress off the concrete floor she looked back to Peter standing idle, "Are you coming?"

"You're distracting me," he replied with a smile.

"Get in the car," she replied, taking his arm.

Reaching the car, Troy stepped forward and opened her door. "Thanks," she smiled.

Blake left the bedroom, feeling more comfortable wearing her casual button-up shirt and jeans. The kitchen and dining room were full of the crews and their wives drinking and eating.

As the night rolled on, one of the wives snuck in a cake, "As you couldn't get your cake made early. I baked this one." A white iced sponge with store-bought confectionery flowers adorned the top. Two small plastic toy firefighters stood above their names. *Cute.*

"Oh, thank you," Blake replied with a hug. She glanced toward Peter; he was playing around with the TV sound system. "Pete, that can wait."

Hand in hand they cut the cake finishing off the wedding photos for the evening. The rest of the evening was partying with everyone leaving around midnight. Alone Blake grabbed her glass of water and dropped down at the table. Flicking through the photos in her inbox. A smile grew on her face. *We have done it.*

Although the photo of the group out the front of the Highgate Station, with her dressed in an evening gown and her captain's jacket and cap was meant to be private, a copy of the newspaper story was on every fire station notice board in the city. A large framed print of the photo hung on Blake's office wall. A reminder of her achievements over the last twelve months. Getting her promotion and finding love in a sea of smoke. Peter had the same idea, sealing his claim to the marriage. He called it Inter-brigade relations.

Arriving at the wildfire deployment wasn't any different to any other year. There were some familiar faces from previous fires. Peter parked his truck beside Blake's engine. Both crews mulled around checking their gear waiting for further directions. They were joined by other firefighter mates. One female firefighter approached the group, "Hey, Peter," wrapping her arms around him with a short hug.

Blake stood across from him listening to a crew discussion. Raising her eyes, her gaze connected with Peter's. He looked so awkward as he pulled away, "Nic," he pointed to Blake, "I'd like you to meet my wife, Blake." With a distant handshake and nod, their introduction was interrupted when the captains were called to the Incident Controller's tent.

"A story for later," Blake whispered as they walked across the field.

"Just a firefighter—"

"Later," Blake butted in as they approached the group.

Blake and Peter stood with the numerous other crew captains waiting for their orders. The incident controller entered the tent giving his briefing. "Captain Sycamore," he looked up as Blake and Peter stepped forward. The controller looked confused for a second, glancing down at his notes, "Captain Peter Sycamore," handing over a clipboard. The controller turned to Blake, "Captain Blake Sycamore?" Still looking confused as her jacket name tag read Davis.

"Just call me Captain Davis," she replied.

Blake jumped aside as a snake slithered away from the slow-burning grass. Numerous crews were backburning the grass paddocks to save a farmhouse and milking shed. Giving the orders and not having to worry about Tim gave this deployment a different vibe. The new rookie had no problems blending in with the team.

Later that day out on the fire ground, Blake tossed a fallen branch aside when a tall stranger approached her through the smoke. As he got nearer a deep cheeky voice said, "Helloo, sexy."

Really. Keeping a straight face her eyes rose to connect with his, "Hello Peter." Pulling out her water bottle she leaned back against an old tractor surrounded by farm equipment, "If you had approached me like that the first time we met, I would have had another assault hearing to deal with."

"Noted," he replied with a smile holding out a bag of caramels.

The End

ABOUT THE AUTHOR

Christine L. Hamilton enjoys writing short stories and novels in the genre of Sci-fi, and Adventure with a romantic subplot. As well as Contemporary Romance works, written to Sweet Romance to closed-door heat level. Currently self-employed as a freelance writer, she creates a range of fiction and non-fiction books. She grew up in outback Queensland Australia and now lives in tropical north Queensland. Living in rural Australia and her twenty-seven-year career in the emergency services gave her a wide variety of experiences which she includes in her story plots. Her works can be found at www.pagesnmore.com.

I hope you enjoyed this book, please leave a review to help others when choosing this book. Thank you.

OTHER BOOKS BY THIS AUTHOR

Christmas Romances 5 Short Stories.

Heartwarming romance short stories where two people find each other and their feelings grow over the festive holidays. The Five Christmas Romance stories are set during Summer in the Southern Hemisphere. The stories are based on workplace, contemporary and hometown romances. This sweet romance is written with mild heat to closed-door, fade to black heat levels. No part of this book is AI-generated. An enjoyable read. **Rated 5 Stars by *Reader Views*.**

If you liked Stranger in the Smoke and want to help me create more, please leave a review and tell a friend. Thank you hope you liked it.

Christine